"Dammit, *Emma! You're driving me crazy, you know that?*

Cash swiveled to meet her gaze, only to get so hung up in it he had no idea how to find his way out again. The words shimmered in the space between them for a moment before fading into the cushiony silence. Finally Emma smiled, a whatcha-gonna-do? curve to her lips that shoved Cash right over the line between *then* and *now*.

"Yeah. Same here." She hesitated, then glided the back of her hand down his cheek, and Cash's breath curled into a hot, dry knot in the center of his chest. "Crazier than I've ever been in my life."

Emma saw Cash swallow, wanted to press her lips to those clenching muscles in his throat, to pull this man inside her—in more ways than one—so badly her own throat went dry.

"Should that be a bad thing?" he finally said.

"Don't know. Don't care…"

Dear Reader,

When Cash Cochran offers to help the widowed Emma
Manning pull her neglected farm back from the brink of
disaster, she might have thought Cash was the answer to
her prayers. But now that I've finished their story, I'm
thinking Emma was far more the answer to Cash's…even
if he didn't know he was asking.

It's probably pretty evident to anyone who's read my
books how often they explore themes of self-worth,
redemption and forgiveness, based on my own deep-
seated conviction that good always ultimately triumphs
over bad. *Welcome Home, Cowboy* goes down those
roads, and then some, with Cash being probably the most
tortured hero I've ever written (Emma definitely had her
work cut out for her!). But, oh, what a joy and privilege
it was—for Emma and for me—to accompany him on his
journey.

I hope you think so, too.

Karen Templeton

WELCOME HOME, COWBOY

KAREN TEMPLETON

SPECIAL EDITION

Published by Silhouette Books

America's Publisher of Contemporary Romance

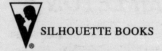

SILHOUETTE BOOKS

ISBN-13: 978-0-373-65536-6

Recycling programs
for this product may
not exist in your area.

WELCOME HOME, COWBOY

Printed in U.S.A.

Books by Karen Templeton

KAREN TEMPLETON

Since 1998, RITA® Award winner and Waldenbooks bestseller Karen Templeton has written more than thirty books for the Harlequin and Silhouette lines. A transplanted Easterner, she now lives in New Mexico with her husband and whichever of their five sons happens to be in residence.

To Gail, for grace and understanding and patience.
My gratitude knows no bounds.

Chapter One

Cash Cochran hadn't known what to expect, but for damn sure goats in coats hadn't made the list.

His breath clouding his face, he frowned at the half-dozen or so beasts in the wire-fenced pen adjacent to the barn, bright-colored balloons on spindly legs. They squinted back with bemused smiles, droopy ears flicking. One gave him a questioning bleat.

I'm not sure, either, Cash thought, his gaze sweeping what had once been a sizable mamas-and-calves operation, sold off in bits and pieces until nothing remained except the house and the ten or so acres his father'd willed to Lee Manning a few years ago…a discovery that'd nearly knocked Cash right off the wagon. Except that was one level of hell he had no wish to revisit, thank you.

Not that he'd needed, or wanted, the property, nestled between two mountain ranges in northern New Mexico. Lee and his wife had been welcome to it. But the *why* behind the bequest had tainted the lapsed friendship with a bitter stink, one time had barely begun to dissipate.

The sun popped out from behind a doughy cloud, bringing changes into sharp relief—the fair-size, utilitarian greenhouse, the unplowed fields, a young orchard not yet in bloom. Tattered, heavy-duty plastic clinging to one side of the house—an abandoned home-improvement project would be his guess. The goats. Even so, the endless sky and pure, weightless air, the wind's contented sigh through the pinon windbreak—those were exactly as he'd remembered.

What he'd missed.

Unlike the house itself—a ranch-style built high enough for a porch but too low for a basement, the exterior a conglomeration of stucco and fake brick and bad siding—which he hadn't missed at all. Putrid memories punched through the paneled wood door and fake-shuttered windows, trampling the riot of egg-yolk-yellow daffodils crowding the foundation, the cutesy Welcome sign beside the recently repainted porch—

Barking its head off, an avalanche on four enormous, filthy feet roared around the side of the house and straight toward Cash.

"Bumble! Heel!"

Cash's head jerked up, his gaze colliding with blue-green eyes as steady as they were curious. The called-off polar bear of a dog swerved at once, trotting over to plant his butt beside the red-sweatered goat his mistress held on to. A jumble of coppery hair, the bright plaid scarf hanging down her front, both glowed in contrast to the blah-colored, too-large barn coat, faded jeans, muddied boots.

"Can I help you?"

"Sorry, ma'am, didn't mean to cause a ruckus. I'm—"

"I know who you are," the woman said with a bite to her West Texas drawl that made Cash wonder if she kept the dog around just for show. At least she'd been smiling in her wedding photo.

"I take it you're…" He scoured his brain for her name. "Emma?"

"That's me."

Cash couldn't remember the last time a woman didn't go all swoony and tongue-tied in his presence. Longer still since such things had stoked his ego, made a lonesome young cowboy with a fair talent for guitar picking and songwriting feel like hot stuff. It'd surprised him, how fast all the attention got old. Especially when it finally penetrated that the gals were far more interested in Cash's so-called fame than they were in him. Still, Emma Manning's obliviousness to his so-called charms unnerved him. His attention swerved again to the goats, still watching him with squinched-up little faces.

"Why're they dressed?"

"Had to shear 'em before they kidded. Then the temperature dropped. Mr. Cochran…I'm sorry, but why are you here? Since I somehow doubt you dropped by to chitchat about my goats."

He glanced back, caught the frown, the fine lines feathering the corners of those cool, calm eyes. "Guess you'd call that a loaded question. Lee around?"

Something flickered across her face—irritation, maybe—before she wordlessly led the goat back to the pen. Hot shame licked up Cash's neck, that if he hadn't found that letter a few months ago—a letter he hadn't realized he'd kept—he might not even be here now. But he was, which was the important thing.

Wasn't it?

Emma gently kneed the goat's rump, encouraging her to rejoin her friends. Her silence, however, was anything but gentle. Even her hair—scattered across her back, nearly to her waist—seemed to crackle with anger. Anger he wasn't totally sure he understood, truth be told.

"I know I should've called first," he said, "but this morning...I just found myself heading out this way. And by that point I figured I'd better see it through before I lost my nerve. If Lee's not here, no problem, I could come back." From inside the pen, puzzled eyes cut to his. "I bought a house a few months ago, on the other side of town. Haven't been there long, though. Couple, three days—"

"You moved back to Tierra Rosa?"

"For the time being, yeah. I guess..." He lowered his eyes, wrestling with this newfangled thing called honesty. Meeting her gaze again, he said, "I guess sometimes you gotta go back to the beginning before you can move forward. And part of that's patching things up with Lee—"

"That's not possible, Mr. Cochran," Emma said quietly, latching the gate before facing him again. "Since Lee died last fall."

If she'd had more than thirty seconds' notice, Emma might've finessed the news a little more instead of blurting it out. Then again, she wasn't exactly feeling too steady on her pins herself, since she'd no more expected to see Cash Cochran standing in her yard that morning than she would've the Lord Jesus.

"I'm sorry," he finally said. "Haven't been in touch with anybody from around here for years. I..." Giving his head a sharp shake, Cash pressed one palm against the SUV's roof, softly swearing as he stared over it. "What happened?"

"His heart," Emma said, refusing to indulge the lingering grief razoring the words. "Apparently it was a substandard model. Like putting a rusty, used-up four-cylinder engine in a semi." She brushed off her hands, rammed them in the pockets of Lee's old barn coat. Willed the fine tremor racking her body to subside. "There was some talk about a transplant, but turns out that wasn't really an option."

"I'm so sorry," Cash repeated on a rough breath, the wind toying with the ragged ends of the hay-colored, shoulder-length hair visible beneath his cowboy hat. "More than I can say."

"Yeah. Me, too."

His jaw pulsing, he yanked open his car door. "I didn't mean to intrude. I—" His fist slammed onto the roof. "Damn."

A couple of the goats bleated, concerned. At Emma's knees, Bumble let out a low growl.

"There's coffee on," she heard herself say, even as she thought, *Please, God. No.* "And pie. Peach. From the tree."

Cash's eyes swung to the lone peach tree down by the front fence. Between the altitude, the crazy northern New Mexico winter and Dwight Cochran's neglect, it was a wonder the thing'd survived at all. Like the man in front of her, she thought on a slight intake of breath. Although the tree looked to be in far better shape than he was.

"Mr. Cochran?"

After a moment, he faced her, his famous silver eyes slightly unfocused. "Come on into the house. Until things settle a bit in your head."

Bumble growled at him, louder this time, all Great Pyrenees machismo. Cash almost smiled. "You don't want me here."

"Wouldn't be at the top of my list, no. But if you're feeling a tenth of what I did when I suddenly found myself a widow a few months back, you're in no fit condition to be driving back down that mountain."

"I can manage—"

"Thank you, but I'm not up for taking that chance. And since my chores aren't going away while we're standing here, I suggest we move this conversation inside."

* * *

Inside.

Cash glanced at the house. The memories leered. Then again, what had he expected?

Lee to be here, for starters. To buffer the pain of coming home, ease Cash through the worst of it. Like he'd always done. A stupid-ass assumption to begin with, considering how shredded things had become between them. How shredded Cash had let them get.

Now it was too late. For apologies, explanations, any of it.

"What's to talk about?"

"Whatever led you here after all this time, I suppose." At Cash's hesitation, Emma said, almost sharply, "I promise you, there's nothing in there that can hurt you anymore." When his eyes snapped to hers, her mouth pulled tight. "Lee told me why you ran off. What your father did to you. Husbands share with their wives, Mr. Cochran," she said to his glare. "Especially husbands trying to make sense out of why their best friend cut them off."

"We were kids. We grew apart. I didn't cut him off—"

"Oh, no? When Lee wrote to tell you about us getting the house, you never wrote back, never returned his calls, nothing. If that's not cuttin' somebody off, I don't know what is."

"And if you know about my father, I think it'd be perfectly obvious why I wasn't exactly overcome with joy when I discovered Lee'd gotten buddy-buddy with the man who'd made my life a living hell—"

"Exactly what did my husband tell you? About *why* Dwight left us the house?"

Acid surged in Cash's gut. "Only that some time after I left, he started working for the bastard. Helping out around the place, stuff like that."

"And?"

"And, what? That was it."

"Oh, Lord," she muttered, then added, "We need to talk," in a tone of voice that said there was more to the story. Half of him wasn't sure he wanted to find out what that was, except...

Except if he'd come for answers, what difference did it make who he got them from?

His eyes touched hers. "How strong you make your coffee?"

"You won't be disappointed," Emma said, then set off toward the house. The dog gave him a *Mess with her and you're dead* look, then plodded behind, only to collapse on the porch, completely ignoring Cash when he passed by.

Cash could only hope his father's ghost would extend him the same courtesy.

"Who's that?" Granny Annie barked at them from her "studio," carved out of one corner of the cramped, perpetually cluttered living room. Cats, coffee cups, painting supplies, art magazines and haphazardly stacked vinyl LPs littered a conglomeration of tables and shelves; from a fifty-year-old hi-fi system, Ol' Blue Eyes crooned loud enough to be heard in Wyoming.

"An old friend of Lee's," Emma yelled back, willing her pulse to settle down as she slapped her coat on the rack, then sloughed off Lee's boots. A cat—The Red One, Emma couldn't be bothered learning all their names, especially since half the time Annie couldn't remember them, either—batted at the end of the scarf, dangling by Emma's knees.

"*Who?*" Annie bellowed, clearly not wearing her hearing aids. Emma did not have the energy for that particular battle right now. Instead, she crossed to the record player and turned down the volume, surprised to find her hand still attached to her arm like normal, considering the recent, major hit to her entire molecular structure.

Man took *intense* to a whole new level. Like radioactive.

"You look familiar." All bones and gumption, the old woman crept closer to their visitor, like a buzzard contemplating fresh carrion. A paint-spattered buzzard with dandelion-fluff hair in sore need of a perm. "Do I know you?"

"You used to, Granny Annie," Cash said, taking her skeletal hand in his. "A long time ago. When Lee and I were kids. I'm Cash."

Annie fiddled with her glasses, large-framed holdovers from the Reagan era. "Cash Cochran? Dwight's youngest boy?"

"That's right," he said, pain flashing briefly in his eyes. "I was so sorry to hear about his passing—"

Annie snatched back her hand, looking like she might smack Cash with the brush. Deaf she might be, but Emma'd put her money on the old gal in a back-alley brawl any day. "He's been gone how long now? And you're only now showing up?" Her thin, wrinkled lips smashed flat, she inched back to the canvas to jab "leaves" on "trees." "Everybody loved that boy. Everybody. Seems to me a *friend* would've at least come to his funeral—"

"He didn't know, Annie. Really." At Annie's if-you-say-so shrug, Emma said to Cash, "Why don't you help yourself to that coffee while I check on my daughter? She's home from school with a cold, nothing serious. I'll be right there."

Then she hightailed it down the hall, stealing a few seconds to deal with the blow of discovering her husband had lied to her. Not to mention escape Cash's eyes. Big, hurting eyes that made a woman want to get inside and tinker. Fix things.

Like she didn't have enough to fix already.

Too bad she couldn't lock up her nurturing instincts as easily as she had her libido. Between widowhood and being pregnant and the farm and everything else, all thoughts of hanky-panky had been shoved into a locked file drawer marked "Expired." But her chronic attraction to the brokenhearted? To the grave, baby. To the grave.

She'd long since given up trying to figure out her penchant for the tired, the poor, the huddled masses yearning to break free of whatever put expressions like that on their faces. Lee had razzed her about it all the time, even as he said that was why he loved her, because her heart was even bigger than her butt.

A comment only Lee could have gotten away with, she mused, pausing outside Zoey's door. Lee, who'd also always wanted to make everybody happy. Even if that meant—in his case—keeping one or more parties in the dark.

Leaving Emma with the tidying up.

Thinking, *So what else is new?* she finally peeked through Zoey's partially open door into an explosion of sour-apple green and bubble-gum pink. A conglomeration of skinny appendages, freckles and wayward hair, her daughter was drawing, sprawled on the rag rug Annie'd made for her when she was a baby, in the same colors that had inspired the prissy color scheme. Beside her towered a mountain of used pink tissues, like blobs of cotton candy.

"How're you doing, baby? And throw those tissues in the garbage."

"They're yucky."

"Which is why *you* get to throw them away. Not me."

With a sigh strong enough to rustle the offending tissues, the child gathered them up, then stood and dumped them into her trash can, decorated with a big-eyed Disney princess. "Is the man gone?"

Apprehension curled in the pit of Emma's stomach. Not eagerly anticipating the upcoming conversation, nope. "How'd you know about him?"

"Saw him out the window." Blue eyes, no less sharp for their wateriness, shot to Emma's. "Who is he?" she croaked, like a baby bullfrog.

"An old friend of your daddy's. And keep your voice down, he's right in the kitchen."

"How come?"

"Because he and I have stuff to talk over. Grown-up stuff."

Zoey sniffed out a put-upon sigh, a trait she'd perfected by two, before blowing her nose again. "He looks like that guy Daddy used to listen to all the time on the country music station."

"That's because he is."

Eyes popped. "You serious?"

"Yes. And no, you can't tell anybody."

"Is he gonna stay?"

"Here? No, of course not. He's got his own place." Emma paused, briefly considering the weirdness that was Cash Cochran moving back to Tierra Rosa. "He used to live here. In this house, I mean."

"No way!"

"Yep."

Pale eyebrows pushed together. "He doesn't want it back, does he?"

"I highly doubt it. And even if he did, it's ours now. Nobody can take it from us." At least, that was the plan. "You want more juice?"

"No, I'm good," Zoey said, handing Emma her empty glass before flopping back onto her tummy on the rug, like she didn't have a care in the world. Considering how attached Zoey'd been to her daddy, the child must've inherited Emma's fake-it-till-you-make-it gene. However, her recent disposition to inviting in every cold virus that passed through town led Emma to suspect she wasn't over her daddy's death nearly as much as she let on.

"Hey," Emma said. Zoey looked up. "Love you."

That got a holey smile in response. "Love you, too, Mama."

Releasing a breath, Emma tromped back down the hall to discover Cash—clearly not inclined to stay where he'd been put—standing in her tiny dining room, his fingers curled around a mug, staring at the sixteen-by-twenty J.C. Penney photo special taking up a good chunk of the paneled wall by the window.

"This is real nice," he said, in the manner of somebody who realized he'd missed out on a thing or two.

Emma forced her eyes to the portrait, even though it made her heart ache. Lee'd gone on Weight Watchers the year before; he'd been so proud of how much he'd slimmed down he'd insisted they get their picture taken. Although *slimmed* was a relative term. For both of them. Now, though, she was glad she'd shoved her pride where the sun don't shine and done what Lee'd wanted. Aside from their wedding album, it was the best picture she had of him. If she'd had any part in making him as happy as he seemed in that picture, she supposed she'd done okay.

Sure, she was ticked that Lee'd skirted the truth about what he'd told Cash, but no doubt he had his reasons. He always did. She sighed over the dull pang that became fuzzier around the edges every day. Heaven knew neither of them was perfect, but they'd been good together. Real good. The kind of good a smart woman knew better than to expect more than once in her lifetime—

"Your boy—he okay?"

Wrapped in his father's arms from behind, Hunter beamed his customary infectious grin at the camera, his glasses crooked as usual. But how could she have forgotten, even for a moment, that the rest of the world saw "normal" through a completely different lens than she did? That to most people her boy's slanted eyes and thick neck and fine hair defined him in a way that provoked either pity or discomfort, if not both. If Cash was feeling either of those things, though, she couldn't tell.

Emma smiled. "He's doing great. Nobody gets a bigger kick out of life than Hunter. A life that's perfectly normal. For him. Us, too."

When she turned, Cash's eyes were fixed on her belly.

"Yeah, there's another baby in there," she said, going into the kitchen, where she finally unwound the scarf and draped it over the back of a kitchen chair before scooting across the floor toward the pie. At least, in her head she was scooting. In reality she felt like a hippopotamus slogging through hip-high mud.

"Didn't know this one was coming until a couple of weeks after Lee died. It's okay," she said when Cash's brows dipped, signaling the doubt demons to swarm, taunting her about all the responsibilities balanced on her not-quite-broad-enough shoulders. Sometimes she truly wondered how she wasn't curled up in a fetal position herself, sucking her thumb. She flashed him a smile and scooped up the pie. "Everything's under control. Really."

And the sooner she did that tidying-up thing with Cash about his father, the sooner he'd be gone and she could get back to figuring out the rest of her life.

She turned, the pie cradled in her hands, catching the barely banked blend of disgust and horror on Cash's face as he scanned the kitchen. Meaning, most likely, that a few coats of paint weren't doing a blamed thing to eradicate the bad mojo that had not only sent Cash running but had kept him away for twenty years.

Somehow, she highly doubted the truth would, either.

Don't remember this being part of the marriage vows, she thought, setting the pie on the table.

Chapter Two

At least the house smelled good. Damn good. Like strong coffee and baking and that flowery stuff women liked to keep around. But man, being here was doing a number on Cash's head. In fact, as he watched Emma serve up a huge piece of pie, he felt like somebody with ADD was controlling the remote to his brain.

Cats lazed and groomed in the midmorning sunlight splashing across the dull butcherblock counters, the gouged tile floor—old, faded dreams struggling for purchase in a scary sea of color. Orange walls. Turquoise cabinets. Yellow curtains. Hell, even the table was fire-engine red—

"Bright colors help stimulate the brain," Emma said quietly, setting a plate in front of him and licking her thumb. "We did it mainly for Hunter."

"Did it help?"

Through the calm, Cash caught a glimpse of the worry that was most likely a constant companion. "I don't think it hurt," she said with a slight smile, and his heebie-jeebies about being in the house morphed to apprehension about what she wanted to tell him, which then slid into a skin-prickling, inexplicable awareness of the woman herself—

"Let me get you a refill," she said, whisking away his mug.

—which in turn stirred up a whole mess of conflicting feelings, most of which he'd pretty much lost touch with over the years…none of which he was the least bit inclined to examine now. If ever. The weird, inexplicable spurt of protectiveness notwithstanding—even more weird since he doubted there was a woman on the face of the earth who needed protecting less than Emma Manning—he wasn't the protective type.

More than one shrink had told Cash his self-centeredness was a direct outcome of the hell he'd been through, the old survival instinct clawing to the surface of the toxic swamp that had been his childhood. Although how that survival instinct jibed with an equally strong bent toward self-destruction—at least, early on—neither he nor the shrinks could figure out. Other terms got bandied about a lot, too. Trust issues and emotional barriers and such.

A highfalutin way of saying he sucked at relationships.

At least, that was how his last ex had put it, Cash pondered as he watched the dark, rich brew tumble into his mug, in the note she'd left on the custom-made glass-and-iron dining table in their ritzy Nashville condo eight years ago. Yeah, the tabloids had been all *over* that one.

The self-destructive tendencies, Cash had finally gotten a handle on. Mostly. The putting-himself-first thing, however… not so much.

Which was why it was taking everything he had in him not to bolt. From the house, the woman, whatever she had to tell him. But before he could, she slid into the seat across from him with a glass of milk. He met her frown with one of his own.

"Well?"

"Eat your pie first." The brutal, midmorning light showcased the fine lines marring otherwise smooth skin, the faintly bruised pouches cushioning those odd-colored eyes. Not gray or blue or green but some combination of the three. "Cleaning up after my husband wasn't exactly on my chore list this morning. So I'm working up to it. Besides, I don't know you, Mr. Cochran. I have no idea how you're going to react to what I'm about to tell you."

"Sounds ominous."

"It's not that, it's…" She sighed. "Eat. Please."

So he took a bite of the still-warm pie, letting the smooth, tangy-sweet fruit and buttery crust melt in his mouth. "Damn, this is good."

"Thanks." After watching him for a second, she said, "It really doesn't feel any different? Being here, I mean."

"Looks different, sure," Cash said, reaching for his coffee. "Feels different?" He shook his head. "My brain knows my father's not here. That it's been twenty years. But it's like no time's passed at all."

"You still have some serious issues, then?" When he looked over, she shrugged and swept a strand of hair off her face. "I'm not judging. Just trying to get a feel for where you're coming from."

Cash set down his mug. "How much did Lee tell you?"

"That your daddy got religion when you were little. The kind that gets hung up on the hellfire-and-brimstone stuff and kinda misses the memo about loving one another. That he took the 'spare the rod and spoil the child' thing a little too literally."

Despite being oddly grateful for her directness, Cash had some trouble swallowing the last bite of pie. "He also mention how my father made sure I felt like a worthless piece of garbage?"

When Emma didn't answer, he glanced up, seeing something in her eyes that could suck him right in. If he let it. "That, too."

Sitting back, Cash released a breath. "God knows I've tried long and hard to let go of the bad feelings. But apparently the roots run too deep to dig 'em out completely. Like that old yellow rosebush alongside the fence out front."

Emma curved her hands around her glass, smiling slightly. A farmer's hands, blunt-nailed and rough. Strong. An indentation marked where her wedding ring had been.

"Lord, I hate that thing. A thousand thorns to every bloom. Every year, I'm digging up runners, cussing it the entire time. But I swear nothing short of napalm's gonna kill it."

From the living room, Annie got after one of the cats. Her lips still curved, Emma shook her head, then sighed. "When you're a kid, you assume everybody's life is like yours. That since your parents are loving, everyone's are—"

"Trust me, the opposite doesn't hold true. I knew other kids didn't have fathers whupping the 'sin' out of 'em. Knew, because it hadn't always been that way." Cash paused, letting the wave of nausea play on through. "Worse though…" He swallowed, then met her eyes again. "Worse, was that I couldn't understand why my mother never did anything to stop it. Eventually—when I got older, I mean—I realized she was scared to death of him. Of what he might do."

Emma's brow creased. "He abused her, too?"

"Enough." As many times as he'd vomited the story to assorted therapists, you'd think it wouldn't hurt anymore. Wrong. "I never told Lee that part, and he had no reason to guess since he never came over here. I had cause to hate my father, Emma. He was…obsessed, is the only way to put it. That everybody was a sinner and he was the instrument of God's wrath."

"So you ran away."

"I stayed as long as I could, for Mama's sake. But once she died, it was either leave or lose what little self-respect I had left. Not to mention my sanity. This house…it's like you said. It was infected with his craziness. His meanness. I couldn't…I couldn't *be* good enough for him."

Or for anybody, it turned out. Including himself.

Cash stood, carrying the plate and mug to the sink, noticing the full dish rack despite the dishwasher right under it. Taking his cue, he bumped up the faucet handle, squirted dish soap on the plate, into the mug. His throat clogged. "I'd loved him," he said over the thrum of running water, "before the craziness started. And for a long time, all I wanted was for him to love *me* again. Until I realized that wasn't ever gonna happen. Lee…"

The stab was quick, but for different reasons this time. Apparently regret hurt every bit as bad as self-righteousness. The dish and mug rinsed and in the rack, he faced Emma again.

"Lee was the only person who kept me going back then. Hell, Emma…leaving him and our friendship behind nearly killed me. I doubt…" He almost smiled. "I doubt he had any idea how much I worried about him those first few months. Then to find out—" His nostrils flaring, he shook his head. "I felt like I'd been sliced open with a dull knife. Especially since I couldn't make head nor tail of it. Why Lee'd do that to me."

"Then why didn't you ask him?"

Beneath the calm, Cash heard the vexation bubble to the surface. The loyal wife defending her husband. Envy flashed, receded, replaced by anger of his own.

"Maybe I ran away, but the crap my father left in my head came right with me. That I was worthless, that I'd never amount to anything. I'd already been through hell and back by then, more times than I wanted to admit. How I even got a career going…" He punched out a breath. "Frankly, it was a damn miracle I didn't end up dead in a ditch somewhere. Not sure anyone would've cared if I had. Except my manager, maybe."

"You don't mean that—"

"I'd barely begun to get my head screwed on straight when I heard the old man'd died, that Lee'd inherited this place. What he'd done for that to happen. Guess I took it a little hard."

Emma leaned back, rubbing her belly, and Cash thought with a start about that "And?" earlier, when she'd asked him if there was anything else in the letter. There was, but if she didn't know he wasn't about to tell her. Not yet, anyway. Not until he figured out what to do about it.

Obviously, though, she'd meant something else. Something Lee hadn't seen fit to mention, would be his guess. Not that anything would change how he felt. Yeah, he'd come in search of explanations as part of some lamebrained attempt to make sense of his past. Hell, of his present, for that matter. But that was it. Some hatchets were too big to bury.

Emma had gotten up to cover the pie before a big gray tiger cat got to it. She stood still for a moment, then turned, her arms crossed over her bulging belly.

"Mr. Cochran, your father…he really was crazy."

"Tell me something I don't know."

"No, I mean, he was sick. Mentally ill. Some kind of chemical imbalance that made him act the way he did. Only nobody knew about his illness until a couple of years after you left."

For the second time that day, Cash reeled, Emma's words sparking off the wall of hurt and hate he'd kept in perfect repair for most of his life. "What are you talking about?"

"I wasn't here yet—this was before I'd even met Lee—but apparently one Sunday Dwight came to town and kinda crashed the Baptists' church service, ranting and raving and whatnot. I gather it got pretty ugly."

Cash softly swore. "He hurt anybody?"

"No. Scared the bejeebers out of a lot of folks, though, if the way some still talk about it is any indication. Anyway, long story short, he ended up in a state facility. Lee said they tried to find you or your brothers, but it was like all three of you had vanished."

"That was the idea," he muttered. They were both gone now, but even before their deaths they hadn't been close. Not when they'd saved their own butts but couldn't see their way clear to save their baby brother's. If he'd talked to either of 'em more than a handful of times after they'd split, that was saying a lot.

"Once they got Dwight on the right meds," Emma was saying, "he started acting as normal as you or me or anybody." She paused. "When he did all those things to you, said all that stuff…that wasn't your daddy talking. That was the sickness."

"So, what?" he flung at her. "I'm supposed to just say, 'I see,' and forget it ever happened?"

"I'm only telling you what I know. What you do with it is your business."

The rebuke hit its mark. Breathing hard, Cash turned away, grinding his fingers into the back of his neck.

"Anyway," Emma continued, clearly unperturbed, "Lee and his folks were in the congregation that Sunday. In fact,

Lee and his daddy helped the sheriff subdue Dwight, and Lee's folks felt compelled to take responsibility. Because if they didn't, who would?"

Yeah, Lee's parents had definitely had a handle on the whole "Love thy neighbor" thing. Even neighbors nobody else wanted anything to do with.

"Lee'd started down at New Mexico State by that point," Emma said. "And it was some months before the doctors felt Dwight was stable enough—and could be counted on to take his meds—to release him. So he came back here, even if there wasn't a whole lot left to come home to by that point. Still, he needed looking after. Lee's folks did it at first, but after they died, Lee and I took over. At least until Dwight went into a home a year or so later. Place down in Albuquerque. Nothing fancy, but Dwight seemed to like it well enough."

Smoothing the wrinkled flannel shirt over her stomach, she said, "I assume your father left the house to us because we were the closest thing he had to family. But I had no idea Lee'd never told you what was going on."

"Like I said, we weren't in touch—"

"He could've gotten a message to you, if he'd wanted. Somehow. But it wasn't until after Dwight'd left us the place that Lee finally admitted you didn't know. We had words about that, believe you me.

"So, knowing the cat would be out of the bag once the lawyer contacted you, Lee asked him if he'd send along a note of explanation. Again, I assumed Lee had been forthcoming at that point. Clearly I was wrong."

"Why?" Cash lashed out, not even fully understanding the pandemonium threatening to break loose inside him. "Why didn't he just tell me the truth?"

"I don't know," Emma said as a dryer buzzer sounded from the closed-in porch behind them. "At least, not for sure. Um… do you mind? I've got at least four more loads, and if I lose my momentum I'll be doing laundry at midnight."

Bile rising in his throat, Cash watched her disappear into the add-on his father had built before everything went haywire. The splintered plank floor probably bore the imprints of Cash's knees from when he'd been made to kneel for hours, reflecting on his sins. He drew a deep breath and followed her, standing in the doorway.

The warm, cluttered room smelled clean. Sweet. Dozens of Ball canning jars lined the pantry shelves, lined up by their contents' color like a child's crayon box—yellow to red to orange to green—glistening against the bright, white walls… and white tiled floor.

"What do you mean, you don't know for sure?" he asked at last.

The dryer open, Emma pulled out a peach-colored towel, efficiently folding it into fourths. "Like I said, I thought Lee had told you. Although I know your father didn't want you to know about his illness."

"Why not? After all, it gave him the perfect out." At her sharp glance, he sighed. "You may as well know, I'm not a nice person. Not saying I go around kicking puppies or taking people's heads off because I'm having a bad day or anything. I'm not a total SOB. But my milk of human kindness has always run several quarts low. Finding out about my father… it doesn't change anything. Certainly it doesn't make me feel, I don't know…whatever you think I should be feeling."

Another towel clutched to her chest, Emma considered how little the man in front of her lined up with the image she'd carried of him all these years. Of course, nearly twenty years was bound to change a person. She wasn't the same she'd been at sixteen—why would Cash be?

But whereas marriage and motherhood had softened her, made her more malleable, clearly Cash's experiences had produced the opposite effect. She could practically see the accumulated layers of caution hardened around his soul, like emotional polyurethane. And yet, as impenetrable as he thought they were, their translucence still allowed a glimpse of the aching heart beating inside.

"I don't think anything, Mr. Cochran." At his snort, she dumped the folded towel into a nearby plastic basket, then shooed away The Black One before he settled in for a snooze. "Who am I to say what you should be feeling? I didn't go through what you did. Anyway…"

She hauled out the rest of the towels, heaping them on top of the washer. "As I was saying, your father didn't want you to know. According to Lee, once he was in his right mind again and started piecing together what he'd done to you and your mom and your brothers, he was horrified. Ashamed. Didn't matter to him, either, that he hadn't been responsible for his actions back then. I guess he figured what was done, was done. That some things, you couldn't fix."

The towels folded and in the basket, she clanged up the washer lid, transferred the wet clothes to the dryer, slammed the dryer closed, then dumped the next load in the washer. When she went to pick up the heavy basket, however, Cash grabbed it from her.

"Oh! You don't have to do that—"

"Where's it go?"

"Our—my—bedroom."

A shadow flickered across his eyes before he carted the basket to the master bedroom, the soft pastels and thick com-

forter on the king-size bed a far cry from the cold white walls,
brown spread and worn hooked rug from when Dwight still
lived here.

"Looks nothing like I remember."

"That was the idea."

Several beats passed before he said, "Lee still should've
told me. No matter what my father wanted."

"I agree. But…" Separating the towels and bathroom rugs
into three piles on the bed, she spared Cash a quick glance,
then returned to her task. "Lee and I, we had similar child-
hoods in many ways. Loving parents, stable home life, all of
that. But we were both also teased a lot when we were kids.
For being fat—"

"You're not—"

"Oh, for pity's sake," she said on a light laugh, "I'm big as a
house. Especially right now. No sense in pretending otherwise.
And as a kid I was downright roly-poly. Just like Lee." She
looked up, swiping a hunk of hair out of her face. "But he said
you were the only kid who never made fun of him. How you
stuck up for him when the other kids did." She carted clean
towels and rugs into the phone-booth-size master bath, then
returned. "That you gave him the confidence to get his first
girlfriend. In other words, Lee felt he owed you."

Cash's brows pushed together. "You think Lee saw taking
care of the old man as a way to pay me back for being friends
with him? That's nuts. Especially since it kinda worked both
ways. Lee stuck by *me,* even though I was the kid other kids'
parents told them to stay away from. Like what my father had
was contagious."

"Okay, then maybe Lee figured there wasn't any point in
telling you. Because he didn't think the damage could be
undone, either. To ask you to come back, when the wounds
were still so fresh…" She paused. "Would you have? If you'd
known?"

Not surprisingly, he didn't answer right away. Instead he hefted The Big Fat Gray One, who'd been twining around his ankles, into his arms, scratching her under the chin until her purring seemed to swallow the room. Emma took pity on him. "It's okay, you don't have to answer that—"

"I don't know. I mean, I don't much like that somebody else got burdened with looking after him. But back then…" He blew out a breath. "By the time I left, I doubt I would've been much good to anybody. Let alone the man who'd left me in that condition. Which still doesn't answer why Lee didn't tell me the truth after my father died."

"I know," Emma said, sighing. "Especially since he knew how much it would've ticked me off to find out he hadn't."

Cash almost smiled. "I take it you're not one for keeping secrets."

"No, I'm not. Although I suppose I understand Lee's loyalty conflicts. The Christian duty he felt he had to take care of your father versus his high esteem of you. For overcoming everything you did, for making a name for yourself…if you'd been blood kin, he couldn't have been any prouder of you." Other words bunched at the back of her throat; if she'd been as good as her husband, she'd swallow them. But she wasn't, and if she didn't let them out she'd choke. "Although frankly it got a little tiresome, hearing him talk about you all the time like you were some kind of god."

Only the merest flicker of Cash's eyelids indicated her words had hit home. But her husband's constant adulation of his old friend had irritated Emma far more than she'd let on in the name of matrimonial harmony. Yes, Cash had suffered as a kid—what it must've been like for him growing up, she couldn't imagine. But he wasn't a god, he was just a man—a man who'd made, from everything she could tell, some really poor choices along the way.

At some point a person has to stop using the past as an excuse for his bad behavior. Whether Cash had done that by now, she could hardly tell from a single conversation. But he sure as heck hadn't during all those years of her listening to Lee's ballyhooing about how great he was—

The baby walloped her a good one, a little foot trying to poke right through her belly button. Grabbing the bedpost, Emma stilled, slowly breathing through the Braxton-Hicks contractions that inevitably followed.

"You okay?"

"I'm fine," she said when it ended, straightening. "Getting crowded in there, is all."

She gathered the rest of the towels to stuff in the tiny linen closet in the hall; Cash stepped aside, but the space was too cramped for them not to invade each other's personal spaces. Especially as between them they took up enough space for at least four average-size people. Cash was all hard and lean where Lee had been more on the marshmallow side, but still, there was a lot of man there.

A lot.

The towels crammed into the closet, Emma started back toward the living room. Silently, Cash followed her, ducking into the kitchen to retrieve his jacket, his face creased into a scowl when he came back out.

"I didn't ask Lee to put me up on some kind of pedestal, Emma. God knows I didn't deserve to be on one. But if listening to him talk about me got up your nose, then maybe *you* should've said something instead of staying silent for so long. Or does your thing about the truth only work one way?"

As Emma stood with her mouth open, Cash hunched into his jacket and said his goodbyes to Annie, whose only reply was a waved paintbrush over her shoulder. Then he faced Emma again, his eyes all sharp. "That it?"

"I think so, yes. No, wait," she said the second he got through the door. "There's one more thing."

"And what's that?" he said, still scowling.

"After Dwight went into the home, Lee took him a copy of your first CD."

Cash actually flinched. "Now why on earth would he have done that? Considering Dwight destroyed my first guitar."

Emma laid a hand on her belly as old memories, old hurts, darkened his eyes. "I know, Lee told me—"

"Millie Scott gave it to me," he said to no one in particular, palming the porch post. "I was eleven, twelve, something like that. It'd been her son's before he moved away. Gave me all his how-to-play books, too. Took the better part of the summer to get the hang of it."

With a short, dry laugh, he looked back at Emma. "I was so bad when I started, I'd play in the barn so nobody'd hear me. Except one day Dad did." The glimpse of humor vanished. "God knows I'd seen him mad plenty by then, but that was nothing compared with that time. You'd thought he found me…" His face reddened. "Well, I suppose you can fill in the blanks on that one.

"Anyway, he grabbed the guitar, told me to git. Later I found it smashed to pieces in one of the garbage cans. Took another two years before I could buy another one—Mama'd slip me a couple of dollars every week from the grocery money. Bought it one of the rare times she and I went to Santa Fe by ourselves." His mouth stretched. "My first Fender."

"That the one you hid at Lee's?"

"Yep. I think the old man knew. Or at least suspected. Because whenever he felt the need to get in a dig? He brought up how bad I was. That who'd ever want to listen to me, anyway? Cows and horses, maybe, but that was it." His gaze narrowed. "So why on earth would Lee give him my album?"

"Because that wasn't the same man who destroyed your first guitar! Or got off on belittling you. Mr. Cochran," she said when he turned away, shaking his head, "you're not listening—the drugs, the treatment…they banished the monster who'd lived inside your father all those years! Or at least subdued it. And the man left behind, the real man who'd been there along…he listened to the whole album straight through, tears running down his face."

Her arms crossed against the chill, Emma stepped closer, half tempted to smooth a hand across those hard, tense shoulders, half tempted to cuff the back of Cash's head. "Believe me or not, it's no skin off my nose…but your father died a humbled man. And as proud of you as he could have possibly been. I heard him say it myself more times than I can count. He never expected you to love him again, but at the end of his life he loved *you* more than he could say."

Silence shrilled between them for a long moment before Cash said, "Just not enough to let me know."

"Hey. You wanted answers? These are the only ones I've got."

Another second or two of that hard, unrelenting gaze preceded his stalking to his SUV. After much door-yanking and slamming, he gunned the car out of the drive, mud spraying in a roostertail of epic proportions.

Zoey came onto the porch, snuggling up against Emma's hip. "What was *that* all about?"

Good question, Emma thought on a sigh, fingering her daughter's soft, tangled hair. "When I figure it out, I'll let you know."

Although what was there to figure out? she mused as they went back inside. Wasn't like she'd ever see Cash Cochran again. And thank God for small favors.

Because some aggravations, a body does not need.

Chapter Three

Still breathing hard fifteen minutes later, Cash stomped through the front door to the secluded adobe on the other side of Tierra Rosa he'd impulsively bought a few months before, when coming home had—for whatever reason—seemed like a good idea. When, despite how screwed up his past had been, at least it'd been simple.

Or so he'd thought.

Stacks of still-unpacked boxes silently jeered as he strode toward the recently remodeled, no-frills kitchen and a cold Coke; seconds later he stood on the deck off the dining room, overlooking the village tucked up in the valley below.

He took a swig of the soda, forcing air in and out of his lungs until the brisk spring breeze siphoned off at least enough of the tension so he could think. Sort through the hundred thoughts and images ping-ponging inside his head, some real, others imagined: of Lee, the last time he'd seen him, his brown eyes shiny when he clapped Cash on the shoulder and wished

him well; of his father, crying—crying?!—as he listened to
the CD; of the contradiction of compassion and intolerance, of
patient reserve and brutal honesty, that was Emma Manning,
her steady, funny-colored eyes seared into his brain…

Cash gave his head a hard shake, trying to dislodge the
image. Images.

Had he really been looking for answers, or justification
for the resentment he'd been hauling around like a worn-out
suitcase for the past twenty years? And now that he had those
answers…what, exactly, did he intend to do with them?

About them?

About Lee's request?

Gritting his teeth, Cash parked his butt on the deck railing
to lean against a support post, one booted foot on the railing. Now the breeze skimmed his heated face like a mother's
touch. Except instead of soothing, it only further stoked his
anger, that by making it impossible for Cash to stay, his father
had stolen from him the skies and forests and mountains he'd
loved so much.

His home.

His identity, when you got right down to it.

Not that it mattered, really, once his career took off, and
Cash had figured he'd be tethered to Nashville for the rest of
his days, anyway. Well, except during those years where he
was on the road more than he wasn't. "Home" became whatever stage he was on in whatever city, his "family" his band,
the crew. His fans, to a certain extent.

A turn of events he'd been okay with, for a long time. Especially since focusing all that energy on Cash Cochran, The
Star, let him basically ignore the messed-up dude behind the
name. Until Cash eventually realized that he and his music
were becoming obsolete, save for those few diehard fans still
clinging to country's grittier roots.

What came next, careerwise or lifewise, he had no idea. But a few months ago—about the time he'd stumbled across that letter from Lee—it occurred to him returning to *his* roots might give him breathing space to figure it out. Coming to terms with why he'd left, what'd happened between him and Lee, was supposed to have been an added benefit. Who knew that instead of a quick get-in, get-out, get-on-with-your-life scenario he'd be facing a dilemma he never in a million years thought would even be an issue.

There'd been no excuse for what his father had done to him…except maybe there was. Just like Cash had been more than justified in holding a grudge against his best friend, in using the hurts done to him as an excuse for being a lousy human being…except maybe he wasn't. Justified, that was.

He finished off his Coke and crushed the can, banging the mangled aluminum shell against the deck railing as it dawned on him that, in this case, getting answers wasn't the end of the journey, but only the beginning.

"Emma! Em*ma!*"

Moving as fast as the balled-up human being inside her would let her, Emma hauled herself out of the kitchen, drying her hands on the tail of one of Lee's old denim shirts. A blur of excitement or anxiety, Emma couldn't quite tell which, Annie stood at the living-room window, her quilted robe buttoned wrong. Outside, Bumble was doing the guard-dog thing. Inside, cats perched on the window sill and backs of chairs and sofas, ears perked and eyes huge.

"For heaven's sake, Annie, what—"

"You got company."

Frowning, Emma joined her grandmother-in-law at the window.

Oh, for pity's sake.

She tromped to the front door and hauled it open, thinking only an idiot would pay a woman an unexpected visit before 8:00 a.m. Not that she was particularly surprised that Cash'd returned. Well, once the dust—or in this case, mud—had settled and she'd had a chance to mull things over. Something about the way he'd torn out of here yesterday, leaving all those loose ends dangling. But would it have killed him to have held off until she'd at least had a chance to comb her hair?

Then again, why should he care what she looked like? Or more to the point, why should she?

It was a mite warmer than when she'd fed and checked on the goats a half hour earlier, although that wasn't saying much. Huddled inside the soft, worn shirt, Emma stepped outside, just far enough onto the porch to see Cash give last year's flower beds the once-over.

"It's okay, Bumble," she yelled at the dog, who was circling and whining, worried. The dog shot her a *"You sure?"* look, but trotted a few feet away to lie in the dirt, keeping watch over the man surveying what even Emma had to admit was a sorry state of affairs. Shame and frustration washed over her as she saw Cash take in the pile of wood for the new raised beds she had no way of making, the greenhouse in sore need of repair, the three still-unplowed fields that by rights should at least be under cold frames by now, before his gaze swung back toward the spot on the roof where wind had ripped off a patch of loose shingles a few weeks back.

At last he looked at her, eyes narrowed in a face that was all unshaved cragginess underneath a cowboy hat, the shadow like his own personal cloud that tagged along wherever he went. The morning sun glanced off a belt buckle that on anybody else would've looked ridiculous.

"Who's gonna help you fix all this? Get your fields planted?" He nodded toward the goats. "Stay up all night when these gals start having their babies?"

I'll manage, she nearly said, because that was how women were programmed, as if a double dose of X chromosomes somehow endowed them with magical powers to make everything right. To make the pieces fit, no matter how jagged the edges might be.

Except as the sun climbed relentlessly over the horizon, rudely highlighting all the undone stuff blowing raspberries at her, it hit her upside her uncombed head that sometimes the pieces *didn't* fit. *Like when your husband suddenly dies and leaves you with all his work to do, besides yours, except you were already going full tilt before he died and now you're pregnant and the economy sucks and your choice is somehow make it work or give up. But this is your* home *and, dammit, you don't* want *to give up. You want to be strong and invincible—*

"How bad is it?" Cash said.

—and here's this man standing in your yard who in less than ten minutes has figured out what's taken you months to realize:

That, basically, you're screwed.

Emma sucked in a deep breath, shoving aside the panic that always hovered, looking for the weak spot. "Bad," she said, feeling Zoey's arms slip around her thick waist. "I think this is what you call one of those catch-22 situations. I've got seedlings and all started in the greenhouse, but that's the tip of the iceberg. If I don't get things hardened off and in the ground fairly soon, there won't be enough to make good for my shareholders who'll be expecting returns on their investments come summer. Then again, I couldn't sell enough to hire on sufficient help to make up for…for Lee not being here."

Munching on a piece of toast, Hunter wandered out of the house to stand beside her, his backpack slung over one shoulder. "Who's that?" he said, blessed—or cursed—with the ingenuous curiosity of a much younger child. Her mama-radar on full alert, Emma slipped an arm around her son's shoulders, watching Cash for signs of discomfort or awkwardness. Far as she could tell, there weren't any.

"Name's Cash, son. Your daddy and I were friends when we were kids—"

"Cash Coch-ran?" Hunter sucked in a deep breath. "The… sing-er?"

"That's right. Except I'm kinda taking a break right now. So I thought it might be nice to come back home for a while. Think over a few things. And while I'm doing that—" those silver eyes skidded back to hers "—I could lend a hand here."

Now it was Emma doing the breath-sucking, as both kids' gazes locked on the sides of her face. "Excuse me?"

"Not forever, but until you're through the worst of it. At least until the baby comes. I reckon I still know how to fix a fence and make a raised bed. Fix that roof," he added with a nod. "And you tell me what needs planting where, I can do that, too. Don't know much about goats, it's true, but I'm pretty sure I remember how to navigate the back end of a cow. Don't suppose it's all that much different."

Too stunned to cobble together a coherent sentence, all Emma could manage was a strangled, "Why?"

"I have my reasons," Cash said, coming closer. Close enough to see there was a lot more going on behind those eyes than Emma could even begin to sort out. "And I'm guessing you'd probably be more likely to accept my labor than my check." When she started, his mouth pulled into a tight smile. "Although if you'd rather do it that way, so you could hire whoever you wanted…well, I suppose that'd work, too."

"Ma-ma?"

Emma tore her gaze away from Cash's to look into her son's soft brown eyes, his beaming smile. "What, honey?"

"You were right, huh? You said…God wouldn't let us down, that He…al-ways gives us what we need, as…long as we don't tell Him how to do that." Her son's grin broadening, he pointed to Cash. "And look!"

Biting her lip, Emma looked, thinking it would take a whole lot of humility to see Cash Cochran as the answer to her prayers. Because while she had cause to feel bad for the man, she had even more cause to be wary. For her children's sake, if not for her own.

Although she knew better than to trust what you read in the tabloids, it'd broken Lee's heart when he'd seen Cash's photo alongside some sensational headline slapped across the cover of this or that rag in the Walmart checkout, about the stints in rehab, the failed marriages. True, it'd been a while since she'd read or heard anything untoward. But for all she knew, his "people" had simply gotten better at keeping that stuff from getting out. Or, more likely, that Cash had slipped off the paparazzi's radar.

Still, she thought as Cash stood with his arms crossed over his chest, the picture of patience, if she truly believed everything happened for a reason, maybe now wasn't the time to start picking and choosing. A realization that provoked a deep sigh.

"Guess there's no point in pretending I'm not in a bind," she said. "Normally I'd have more help, but this was the spring everybody picked to move or retire or find other work or join the army… It would've been a trick to get everything done, even if Lee was still here. The kids do what they can, but… they're kids. And the midwife more or less ordered me to take it easy for the next couple of weeks. But you don't owe us anything, not your labor and certainly not your money—"

"And maybe I think I do," Cash said, his eyes locked in hers. Then he glanced away, blowing out a half laugh. "God knows, nothing's happening here the way I expected, but…it's been a long time since I've had the opportunity to be of any real use to anybody. And maybe for old times' sake…"

He looked back at her. "It nearly killed me, watching this place die under my father's hand. And I can see what you and Lee started here. How you salvaged whatever was left. I don't know why, but I can't stand the idea of it going under a second time. Any more than you can, I'm sure."

She blinked back the sudden scald of tears. But when they cleared, she caught a glimpse of at least part of what was going on inside his head. Not in any detail, certainly, but enough to sweep aside what few shreds of useless pride she had left.

"You two need to go on," she said to the kids, "or you'll miss the bus. Zoey, no, get your coat, it's still cold. I know, it'll warm up, but I don't want the nurse calling me to come get you in an hour 'cause your nose starts running again. So go on."

While Zoey fetched her jacket, Hunter solemnly marched down the porch steps toward Cash. He extended his hand; Cash took it, the wordless handshake apparently cementing something Emma couldn't begin to understand. Then, grinning, her son trooped back to the porch to pick up his backpack; a second later Zoey streaked from the house and slipped her hand into Hunter's to walk to the bus.

Not until the kids were out of sight, however, did Emma face Cash again. "Why do I get the feeling you want to do this as some sort of penance or something?"

The muscles around his eyes twitched before he crunched across the dead grass to the sagging wire fence edging the neglected flower garden. "I think what I'm aiming to do," he said quietly, skimming one palm over the top, "is erase the bad memories. Or at least exchange some of them for new ones. I don't want the land back, don't even give that a second thought. But I want…"

Turning, he pushed out a sigh. "For twenty years I've been running, from this place, from all the bad stuff in my head. Didn't do me a lick of good. For twenty years I've thought about nobody but myself. That hasn't done me any good, either. Apparently. I've forgotten what it's like to be a real human being, Emma." Another dry laugh. "If I ever knew. So helping you…it would kill a couple of birds with one stone. You need the help, and I need to get back to basics. To somehow return to that time before everything went wrong. To maybe find the kid I once was. Because deep down, I think that kid wasn't so bad, you know?"

His honesty shot straight to her heart. But the hard set to his mouth, the challenge in his eyes, made it more than clear her sympathy would be unwelcome. After a moment, she nodded.

"So what, exactly, are you proposing?"

"My services for…" He rubbed his chin. "Let's say six weeks. Or until you're on your feet again after the baby comes. Sunup to sundown, if you need it."

If history was anything to go by, she'd be on her feet within twenty-four hours of the birth. She'd often imagined herself as one of those pioneer women who pushed out a baby a year with no sweat. "What about your career?"

He let out a little hunh. "I imagine the music world will get along just fine without me for a few weeks."

The baby shifted; Emma rubbed his spine. "If you're sure…"

"I am."

"Then, all right. I can at least offer you three meals a day—"

"No! I mean, thanks, but this isn't about…" Cash looked away. "This isn't about getting close. Nothing personal, but that's part of the deal. You tell me what needs doing, and I'll do it. But that's it."

Emma was tempted to point out that if part of his goal was to rejoin the human race, staying aloof from the family might not be the best way to go about that. Then again, maybe it was just as well, for many reasons. Like, oh, for instance, the kids getting too close. Especially Hunter, who glommed onto everyone he met. Who'd cried for a week solid after his father's death.

"One thing, though," Emma said. "First time you show up drunk or high, you're gone. I absolutely will not tolerate any of that tomfoolery around my children. Understood?"

Cash's jaw dropped for a second before he let out a laugh. "Emma...I swear I've been squeaky clean for more than seven years. Ever since I wrapped my car around a tree on a back road in North Carolina and realized how bad off I was. You've got nothing to worry about on that score, I swear. So...I was thinking you probably want some of these fences repaired first so the critters can't get at the plantings. Or maybe get those fruit trees pruned?"

"You know how to prune fruit trees?"

"Yes, ma'am. First winter after I left, I ended up at a ranch in east Texas. Small operation, everybody did everything. Aside from the cattle, they also had a decent-size orchard. Peaches and pecans, mostly. So I know my way around a pair of loppers." He grinned, and Emma's chest clutched. Seeing that smile on video was nothing compared with seeing it in person. "You can watch me do the first tree, how's that?"

Finally she laughed. She couldn't help it. There were a quadrillion reasons why his being here was a bad idea, but none of them trumped her relief that the cavalry had apparently arrived.

"When can you start?" she asked, and the grin brightened to the point where it nearly sparkled. Oh, dear.

"I take it there's tools around here somewhere?"

"In the shed behind the greenhouse. Mr. Cochran—"

"And you can forget that 'Mr. Cochran' stuff," he said softly. "Name's Cash."

"Cash, then," Emma said, having no idea why she was blushing. "Thank you."

"You're welcome," he said with a short salute, then strode off, leaving Emma to wonder what she'd gotten herself into. Not to mention what on earth had gotten into Cash. She went back inside to find Annie, dressed now, feeding cats in the kitchen. The old woman looked up from the writhing, furry mass meowing at her feet as she dumped something stinky into a large, flat bowl.

"I take it we've got us some help?"

"How do you know that?"

"Turned my ears on high," Annie said, tapping one hearing aid as Emma lowered herself onto a kitchen chair. "Heard everything clear as a bell. Especially through that pathetic excuse for a window. Wind leaked through my bedroom window so bad last night I thought I'd freeze." Carefully she bent over to set the plate on the floor, dodging the feline swarm attacking it. Much hissing and swatting ensued. That, Annie ignored. Emma's conflicted expression, however, she didn't. "You havin' second thoughts?"

"Heh. God knows we need the help, but I don't need the complications. And trust me, Cash Cochran is the definition of complicated."

Annie poured herself a cup of coffee, poured in a hefty helping of cream and three spoonfuls of sugar, then shuffled over to sit across from her. The Red One immediately jumped up into her lap, giving Emma a smug kitty grin.

"Honey," Annie said, over the cat's slit-eyed, Ohmigodyes! purring when she started scratching his head, "God made humans complicated to keep himself amused." At Emma's groan, the old woman leaned over to grasp her hand, her expression earnest. "That young man *needs* us, Emmaline. Probably a lot more than we need him."

Yeah, Emma thought on a sigh. Exactly what she was afraid of.

Another few days, Cash thought, squinting at the fruit trees as he yanked on a pair of heavy-duty work gloves, and it would've been too late to prune them. Waiting until April was pushing it as it was; any farther south, they would've already bloomed by now. But the stubborn winter had actually worked in Emma's favor, keeping the trees dormant.

Almost like they'd been waiting for him.

Oh, hell, *no,* Cash thought as he hefted the pole saw and trudged across the muddy field to the first tree. Destiny, fate, divine intervention, whatever you wanted to call it…nothing but people's ways of trying to find purpose in coincidence.

"I could die a happy man," he said to the giant dog, who'd tagged along—out of boredom, Cash supposed, "if I never heard 'It was meant to be' ever again."

The dog seemed to shrug, then plunked down in the dirt where he could keep one eye on the goats. Or ear, maybe, since his eyes closed almost immediately.

The high, bright sun quickly burned off the morning's chill; by ten Cash had shucked both his jacket and long-sleeved shirt. By noon sweat plastered his T-shirt to his back and chest, even though it was probably barely above sixty degrees. But at seven thousand feet there was a lot less atmosphere to buffer the sun's rays.

And absolutely nothing to buffer his thoughts as he cut out the dead wood, opening up the trees to coax a better yield. It'd been ages since he'd worked this hard. No doubt he'd be paying for it tomorrow, he thought as he took a break for another swallow of now-warm water from a liter-size bottle, in time to see Emma headed his way with a towel-covered plate and a thermos.

"What's that?"

"Food." She stripped the towel from the plate to reveal a couple of sandwiches, an apple, another piece of pie. "One's leftover ham from Sunday's dinner, the other's peanut-butter-and-jelly. Since I didn't know what you liked."

"I thought I said—"

"You said you didn't want to eat with the family. Not that I couldn't feed you. Oh, and that's sweet tea. Annie insisted I bring you some."

Cash's stomach growled. He'd figured on going back into town to get something, but refusing her offering would be rude. Not to mention dumb.

"Thanks," he said, removing the gloves to take the plate. "Appreciate it."

"I used mustard on the ham, I hope that's okay—"

"It's fine. Picky, I'm not."

One side of her mouth lifted. "You want me to leave?"

And, oh, he wrestled with that one for a good long while. Because God knew he really was in no position to be forming attachments. Especially with his best friend's widow. But, damn, it'd been forever since he'd simply enjoyed the company of another human being. At least, not without there being a million strings attached.

"No, it's okay, you can stay. I guess."

Cash realized his mistake the instant humor sparkled in Emma's eyes. She tried to wrap up more tightly in a long sweater that didn't come anywhere near to covering her belly. "Should I feel honored?"

"Doubt it," he said, and she laughed. A rich, from-the-belly laugh that took him by surprise. Still chuckling, she surveyed his work, nodding in what he took for approval. She'd combed her hair—it'd been a tangled mess before, probably because he'd shown up earlier than was socially acceptable—but instead of leaving it down she'd bunched it all up at the back of her head in a sloppy bun. If it hadn't been for the freckles, or her eyebrows being nearly the same color, he wouldn't've believed that color red really existed in nature. But somehow he didn't see Emma as somebody who faked anything, least of all her hair color. He found it hard not to stare at it.

To stare at her.

He lowered himself onto a dry patch in the dirt underneath one of the bigger apple trees, chomping off a huge bite of ham sandwich. Even through the tart burst of mustard, he could taste the sweet-smoky, thickly sliced ham. Damned if that didn't take him back, too. But not to the bad times, to a place before that. A place he'd missed.

Emma twisted around, a soft smile on her lips. A piece of hair had worked loose, curling lazily around her cheek. She shoved it behind her ear. "Looks good."

"Thanks. Should be finished by the end of the day. Figured I'd get to those fences tomorrow, then start on the raised beds the day after, if that's okay."

"That'll be fine. I've already started hardening off the greenhouse plants, so they'll be ready to go in the ground in a few days."

"What all you planting?"

"Bit of everything. Broccoli, beans, several kinds of squash. Melons. A lot of lettuces. Those sell really well, especially to a couple of local restaurants that buy from us. Our CSA clients really like 'em, too."

"CSA?"

"Community Supported Agriculture. Otherwise known as farmers' angels."

Emma moved to a small stone bench nearby, slowly easing herself onto it with a soft groan. The dog roused himself and trotted over, nudging her hand until she shoved her fingers into his thick fur.

"You okay?"

"Yeah, fine. But…as much as I love being a mama, the last month of pregnancy is the pits. Cramps my style. And this one clearly thinks he's in a lap pool." She hesitated, then said, "I think this is what you call irony. Lee and I wanted a batch of kids. But we'd figured, when only two showed up in nearly thirteen years of marriage…I honestly thought we were done." She shrugged. "Surprise."

"You regret the timing?"

"That Lee won't get to see this one? That my baby won't ever know his daddy? Of course I do," she said, shifting. "Every single day. Lee's dying was definitely not part of the plan. But having this little guy to look forward to…" He saw her eyes glitter before she lowered them to the dog, now prone on the ground beside her. "It's definitely taken some of the sting out for Hunter and Zoey. For me, too. Silver linings and all that."

"You know it's a boy?"

"Yeah. The kids and Annie and I argued about a name for months." She smiled. "Finally settled on Skye."

"Skye Manning. Good name." Cash lowered his eyes to the half-eaten sandwich, waiting for the unidentified feeling to pass. "Bet Lee was a great father."

Emma laughed again. "Oh, he stumbled around in the dark about parenthood like any other human being. Loving your kids doesn't mean you know what you're doing. But yeah. He was. The kids were crazy about him. Hunter, especially…he simply couldn't make sense of Lee's death. And he's pretty philosophical about most stuff. But he was so *angry*…" Biting her lip, she averted her gaze.

"Like his mama," Cash ventured, and a tight smile curved her mouth. She heaved herself around to get up, startling the dog to his feet, too.

She regarded the orchard for a moment before asking, "Did you know about Lee's heart condition?"

"No," he said around the rest of the ham sandwich, then scooped up the piece of pie. "I remember him being out of school a lot, always having doctors' appointments. But that was when we were still pretty little. Elementary school. I don't recall any problems past that point. Other than the usual, I mean. Colds, the flu, stuff like that. So you're saying this wasn't sudden?"

"For me, it was," she said, then sighed. "I'll spare you the medical terminology—which I could never pronounce right, anyway—but something about his heart made proteins slowly build up in his organs. The upshot was, by the time he had his little 'episode,' his kidneys were basically gone, which meant he wasn't even a candidate for a heart transplant. I think he knew his days were numbered. He just didn't know what that number was. And for some reason he didn't feel I was on the need-to-know list."

"It wasn't right, him not telling you."

Cash wasn't sure which one of them his vehemence startled more. But it all seemed so stupid. And wrong, and unfair. Lee's misguided belief that hiding the truth was somehow kinder than being honest, his dying so young, all of it.

"At the time," Emma said, "I would've agreed with you. And I'll admit it still rankles, sometimes. Then I think…what if I had known? Would I have still married him? Absolutely. But would I have said okay to having kids? To taking on this farm?"

A few more pieces of hair escaped when she slowly shook her head. "I don't know. I'm pretty good about taking things as they come, but I'm also practical. Not a big fan of starting things I can't finish. Then again, I can't imagine life without my kids. Without this place," she said, sweeping out one hand. "Any more than I can imagine what my life would've been like without Lee in it."

The pie gone, Cash wiped his hand on his jeans. "Even though—"

"Yes, even though he kept secrets from me. Even though he never cleaned off his boots when he came inside the house, or put the top back on the peanut butter, or that he played a certain country singer's CDs over and over to the point I thought I'd lose my mind," she added with a devilish glint in her eyes. "Human beings drive each other nuts sometimes. So what? Lee *loved* me, and his kids, and the life we'd made together. And he was a good man, the kind of man a woman's proud to have by her side. So no real regrets. Except for the selfish part of me that wishes he'd stuck around a little longer."

A flush of something akin to envy washed over Cash as he picked up the PB&J. Envy, and a dull, reawakened sense of hopelessness he hadn't indulged in a long time. Not about Emma, but for what she and Lee had obviously had. Although to be truthful, considering how badly he'd botched his own relationships, it all sounded like far too much work, if you asked him.

Besides, women like Emma—the kind of woman who saw her man's imperfections but still loved him anyway—were pretty damn rare, in his experience. Then it hit him, how his mother had stuck by his father, no matter what, and look how that had turned out.

He bit into the sandwich; a burst of sweet fireworks went off in his mouth. Chewing, he peeled up the top layer of bread to see generous chunks of fruit embedded in ruby-red goo. "This homemade?"

"Yep. Strawberry preserves. Annie's specialty. We sell a lot of those, too. Especially to a couple of the local B and Bs. Peach, raspberry, blueberry. Cherry. Hot-pepper jelly, too."

"Lord, I haven't had that in years."

"Doesn't work real well with peanut butter, though," she said, and Cash felt a grin shove at his cheeks. Then he frowned again. "How the hell are you so calm? I know how hard it is to work a farm," he said, dodging the inevitable platitude. "Even with help. And you've got two other kids, and Annie—"

"I'm well aware of my obligations without you listing them for me," she said in that maddeningly even tone. "I'm not in denial. Never have been. But like I said, I'm good at taking things as they come—"

"And what would've happened if I hadn't shown up?"

"But you did."

Keeping the apple for later, Cash got to his feet and handed her the empty plate. "Okay, then what about when I leave? What then?"

The plate clutched in one hand, Emma crossed her arms over her belly. "If you walked away right now and we never saw you again, I'd still be ahead of where I was yesterday. You pruned my fruit trees," she said, nodding toward the orchard. "One less thing for me to worry about. Look, I'm grateful for any help I can get. Whatever your motives, I'm not proud. Well, I am, but not too proud to accept assistance—"

"And you still haven't answered my question. How are you going to manage?"

"I have no idea. But I will. Somehow." She shrugged. "It's called trusting that things will work out. Like they always have."

The obvious spiritual undertone grated. Not that Cash cared one way or the other what, or who, people chose to believe in, but far as he could tell the only thing a person could count on was himself.

"You don't have doubts?"

A short laugh erupted from her mouth. "Oh, honey, I've given them names, they hang around so much. I didn't say it was easy, trusting that hard. I also didn't exactly shrug and think, *Whatever,* when Lee died, believe me. But wrestling with the doubts is what keeps me from getting too big for my britches." She almost smiled. "Although I guess it's been too late for that for some time."

Then she walked away, her hair blazing in the sun no match for her radiant dignity. Of course, all that stuff about trusting was a crock. Far as he could tell life was more or less about making sure you were smarter and faster than the other guy.

But he had to hand it to Emma—she sure talked a good talk. In fact, for a second or two there, she almost had him listening. Nowhere near believing—hell, no—but listening was the crucial first step, wasn't it?

Yeah. The first step, Cash thought as he went after a branch like it'd personally offended him, down a road that led to nothing but disappointment and heartache.

A road he had no intention of ever going down again. Not in this lifetime, or any other.

Amen.

Chapter Four

"Mama!" Zoey yelled, stomping through the front door, soooo glad this totally, completely stinky day was over. She'd forgotten her spelling homework, lunch had been some disgusting sandwich she couldn't even eat, and jerkface Jaxon Trujillo would *not* stop bugging her. And then she tripped getting off the school bus so she landed on her hands and knees in the dirt, and all the kids still on the bus laughed at her. Not even Bumble's sloppy kisses when she hugged him made her feel better. "I'm home!"

"Shh, child, your mama's taking a nap," Granny Annie said as Zoey wriggled out of her backpack and let it thud to the floor. Except Granny gave her one of her looks, so she picked it back up and hung it on the peg by the door as she was supposed to. "Tryin' to, anyway. Where's your brother?"

"It's Thursday. He always stays after school to work with Miss Winnie, remember?"

"Oh, that's right, I forgot. There's a snack on the kitchen table. Then come look at this painting, tell me what you think."

A bunch of cats followed Zoey into the kitchen, where she sighed. Peanut butter graham crackers. Blech. Mama's cookies and cakes and stuff were *scrumptious,* but Mama'd said she couldn't bake too much right now on account of the baby made it hard for her to stand for very long.

Which made Zoey feel all tight inside if she thought about it too hard, so she didn't. Especially since Miss Rollins, her Sunday-school teacher, had told her it wasn't—she wrinkled her nose, trying to remember the word—*charitable* to think about herself when Mama had so much on her mind. But she'd sure be glad when the baby was on the outside and she could have Mama back, and she didn't care who knew it.

Well, except for Miss Rollins.

She carefully poured herself a glass of milk, nibbling on one of the crackers while she watched, through the kitchen window, Cash talk to the goats as he fixed their fence.

Zoey could hardly wrap her head around Daddy and Cash being friends. They were just *so* different. Like, for instance, Daddy smiled all the time, where Cash mostly looked like he had a stomachache or something. But then, Daddy always had something good to say about everybody. Even people who did bad things, he'd say they were probably like that because nobody had ever shown them how to be good. That if they knew how to be better, they probably would be.

With lots of clanging, Cash dropped the tools into Daddy's beat-up old metal box and headed back to the greenhouse. He certainly *seemed* normal enough. At least when he talked to the goats. But she got the feeling he liked them better than he did people. And that was just wrong.

Carefully holding the glass of milk and two graham cracker sandwiches, Zoey tiptoed past Granny—even though she couldn't hear her, anyway—down to Mama's room to peek in. She was lying on her side on the big bed, her hand over the ginormous lump where the baby was, frowning in her sleep. Except then she said, "I know you're there, Jelly Bean, you may as well come on in," so Zoey went over and kissed her forehead. Then she brushed off the graham cracker crumbs, and Mama laughed and pulled her up onto the bed beside her to lie down, all curled around the baby.

Zoey squirmed. "It tickles when he moves."

"You should feel it from the inside. Like he's making pizza dough." Smiling, Mama smoothed back Zoey's crazy hair, which was all curly, like Daddy's. Mama's hair was smooth and shiny over her shoulders, and she smelled like the fancy candles at Hobby Lobby. But sometimes it felt hard to breathe from Mama's loving her and Hunter so hard, like she wanted to make up for Daddy being gone.

"How was school?" Mama asked, like she did every day, and Zoey shrugged and said, "Okay," because she wasn't gonna tell Mama about her troubles. Because that wouldn't be charitable, either, probably. Although if Jaxon Trujillo called her barfhead one more time, she was gonna pop him one. Maybe.

Mama pushed herself up, stealing one of Zoey's graham cracker sandwiches and taking a big bite. "Hey!" Zoey said, giggling, then remembered she did have *some* good news. She stuck her fingers in her mouth and shoved up her top lip. "'Ook!"

"Hallelujah, it's about time." Mama wiped her crumby hands on her jeans and put her hands on both sides of Zoey's face to open her mouth wider. "Looks like they're coming in straight, too, praise be. Okay, move over, punkin'—I gotta pee."

After Zoey scooted out of the way, Mama got up and slowly walked into her bathroom, half shutting the door so Zoey couldn't see her do her business. "When I got off the bus," she called, "Cash was fixing the goats' fence."

"Really? I didn't think he'd get anywhere near that today—"

"He was talkin' to 'em, too."

Mama laughed the same time the toilet flushed. Then she pushed open the door, watching Zoey in her mirror as she brushed her hair. "We all talk to the goats, what's so strange about that?"

"But we don't talk *only* to the goats."

Mama twisted her hair into a big old curled-up snake at the back of her head, then stuck a giant barrette in to hold it. "Cash talks. When he wants to. He just prefers to keep to himself."

"How come?"

"I suppose you'd have to ask him that."

Zoey pushed out a breath. How was she supposed to ask him anything if he didn't talk? Honestly. "Do you think he's happy?"

Mama came back into the bedroom, rubbing lotion into her hands. "Where on earth did that come from?"

"I don't know. I don't ask for this stuff to show up in my head, it just does."

Laughing real softly, Mama sat back on the edge of the bed. "No," she said, hugging Zoey's shoulders. "I don't think Cash is happy at all."

"That would be my take on it, also," she said, then frowned. "You'd think, with him being famous and rich and all, he'd be smiling all the time."

"Oh, honey," Mama said, her breath warm in Zoey's hair. "Being famous and rich might make you feel good for the moment, but if you don't feel right on the inside, nothing on the outside is going to make you really happy."

"And Cash doesn't feel right on the inside?"

"No," she said quietly, like she'd been thinking about it, too. "A lot of bad stuff happened to him when he was a kid, and that's left him with a whole bunch of confusing thoughts he's having trouble sorting out. It's like…he's spent so long staring at what he thinks he sees, he can't see what's really there."

Zoey wasn't even gonna try to figure that one out. Instead, she said, "Daddy said you were real good at helping people see the light. So maybe you should give Cash a shot."

Mama made a funny choking sound, then said, "Unfortunately, that only works if the person wants your help. Cash wants…" Her forehead all pinched together, she combed her fingers through Zoey's messy hair. "Actually, I'm not entirely sure what he wants. But it's not my help. And anyway, he's only here until after the baby comes—"

"But if Daddy was Cash's friend, don't you think he would've wanted us to make Cash feel better?"

"Except we don't know Cash like Daddy did—"

"But aren't we supposed to love everybody, even if they don't love us?" Except maybe for Jaxon Trujillo. Zoey thought probably even the Lord Jesus might have trouble with that one. "Maybe Cash just needs somebody to love him. Like Charlie Brown's Christmas tree."

That made Mama laugh again. "Very true, Miss Smarty Pants. But you can love somebody without getting in their face about it. And to be honest, I've got enough to think about right now without taking on somebody else's troubles. But I'll tell you one thing…his showing up right now couldn't've come at a better time. Like Hunter said, he's an answer to a prayer. Oh, there's Granny calling—you better scoot."

With that, Mama quickly kissed Zoey on the mouth and shooed her out of the room before Zoey said something stupid. Like how Cash was the strangest answer to a prayer she'd ever heard tell of, and that was the truth.

Then she went out to the living room where Granny's sun-catchers in the windows threw rainbows all over the walls, and her painting was all happy and colorful, even if Zoey didn't have a clue what it was supposed to be, and two of the kitties ran over to be petted, and she could barely remember why she'd thought the day was so stinky.

Sure, she missed Daddy, and she knew they didn't have a lot of money to "throw around," as Mama said, but it wasn't like the world had ended or anything when he died. Also, she *knew* if Daddy was here he'd do something to make Cash feel better.

Then Hunter walked through the front door, grinning in that way that always made Zoey feel good. He went over to hug Granny, then Zoey, like he hadn't seen her in a million years, and Zoey got one of her Bright Ideas.

"You busy, Hun?"

"Uh-uh," Hunter said, wagging his head. "What's…up?"

"Then come with me," she said, taking him by the hand and leading him back outside.

Because this was what Daddy would have wanted, she was sure of it.

Cash heard the kids before he saw them, bearing down like a pair of giggling, heat-seeking missiles, the dog plodding alongside as though mildly annoyed at being called to action.

He tensed. A kid person, he wasn't. Never had been. Kids moved too fast, talked too much, and asked way too many questions. He supposed there'd been a time when he might've thought about having children of his own, but that moment had passed a loooong time ago, never to return. Especially once he realized he'd make as lousy a father as he had a husband.

So he been more relieved than offended when Emma pretty much indicated she'd rather he stayed away from her babies. Not that she'd told him that to his face, but he'd gotten the message clear enough. He was guessing she had no idea they'd come to see him now.

"Hey, Mr. Cochran!" the girl said, her hair even brighter than her mother's. Her smile, too. She wasn't what you'd call a pretty child, but Cash'd wager those eyes alone would have the boys falling all over themselves in a few years. "Hunter and me thought it was high time we properly introduced ourselves."

Her odd, too-grown-up speech made Cash's mouth curve in spite of himself. "Except we've already met. At least, Hunter and I have." He turned to the boy, short for his age, his hooded gaze almost startling in its directness. "Isn't that right, Hunter?"

"Zo-ey made me come with her. But Ma-ma said we were sup-posed to leave you a-lone."

"No, Hunter, she said we weren't supposed to *bother* him," Zoey said, then turned a gap-toothed smile on him especially designed to melt hearts. If those hearts were meltable to begin with. "But we're not bothering you, huh?"

Yes, you are, now git, he half wanted to say. Except the words weren't in Cash's voice, but in his father's. And maybe his head needed about a million more twists before he got it screwed on straight, but he'd hack off a limb before he replicated his father in any way, shape, form or fashion.

"Not at all," he said, squatting to pet the dog, who in turn gave him a *Thanks for understanding* shlurp across his face. Then he nodded toward the torn-up side of the house. "What happened here?" he asked, in sore need of a conversation topic.

"Dad-dy was gonna make Gran-ny her own room to paint in," Hunter said, then rubbed his hand across his nose. "Only then he died."

Out of the corner of his eye, Cash saw Zoey slip her hand into her brother's before she looked back up at him. The smile was gone. "He even bought all the wood and everything," she said.

"That why there's all that lumber in the barn?"

"Yeah." Then the grin popped back out like the sun. "Can you fix it for us?"

"What? Oh, no, sorry, guys—that's way out of my league. But I bet I could find somebody to do it—"

Both kids shook their heads. "Ma-ma says we don't have enough money to fin-ish it," Hunter said.

Zoey sighed. "Or even fix it back up the way it was."

Behind them, one of the goats bleated, like she was annoyed at being left out of the conversation. Grateful for the interruption, Cash walked back over to the pen, Emma's spawn trooping along behind. Bumble, too, but not like his heart was in it.

"Mama says they're all gonna have their babies soon," Zoey said, digging in her hoodie pocket for something, which she shared with her brother. "Peanut butter graham crackers," the little girl said in answer to Cash's unspoken question as she and Hunter both poked their offerings through the wire fence to eager recipients. "They eat most anything, but cookies are their favorites. Mine, too."

"Do you like cook-ies, Cash?" Hunter asked, his ingenuous grin even more infectious than his sister's.

"Sure. Who doesn't?"

Zoey's head snapped around. "What's your favorite?"

"Can't rightly say. Chocolate chip, I guess."

"Same here."

Hunter tugged on Cash's sleeve. "I like it when you sing and play the gui-tar."

"Oh. Thanks."

"You're wel-come." Shifting from foot to foot, he said, "Ma-ma says you and Daddy useta be real good friends."

"We were. A long time ago. When we were kids."

Soft brown eyes grazed his. "You miss him?"

Cash smiled. "Yeah. I do."

"Me, too. Dad-dy was the *best*—"

"What on earth are you two doing out there?" Emma called from the porch, and everybody including Cash swung their heads around. "I apologize," she said, heading toward them, "I told them not to bug you—"

"They weren't," he heard himself say, surprised to discover he meant it. Mostly. Not that he was eager to repeat the experience, but he'd lived through it.

"Thank you," Emma said, coming closer, "but this is about being obedient." She tried to give Zoey what Cash assumed was a stern look, although he thought maybe there was more of an *And what exactly are you up to, anyway?* glint to it. "Mr. Cochran's not here to be your buddy, or your playmate. So you both march yourselves right back inside. Now."

The kids dutifully followed orders, although not before Zoey give him a little wave and another grin. "Little turkeys," Emma muttered.

"They were just bein' kids, no harm done." Although truth be told, it wasn't only the kids he'd been avoiding. For reasons all too clear when Emma's chagrined eye roll, then chuckle, ignited a small but potent flame in the center of his chest.

Almost flustered, Cash nodded toward the goats, their eyes blissfully narrowed against the warm sunshine. "I assume they have names?"

Emma pressed a hand to her chest. "I'm *so* sorry—where are my manners? That's Peony begging through the fence, Mimosa beside her. The littlest one's Sweet Pea." She pointed. "Wisteria's in purple, Jasmine's in yellow. And Begonia's the hussy in red. Her Indian name is Escapes Whenever She Can."

Cash felt a grin coming on. "Girly enough names?"

"Was hardly gonna call 'em Butch and Mack."

"Good point. I'm not sure, but I think a couple might be about ready to kid."

He could feel her go instantly on alert. "Which ones?"

"Begonia and…Jasmine?"

Emma carefully opened the gate, blocking Begonia when she tried to make a break for it. "Oh, no, you don't, missy. Can't tell you how many times I've found her at my back door, looking like she's expecting me to invite her in for tea."

"Isn't that what the dog's for?"

"He's a guard dog, not a shepherd." Half squatting, she shoved aside the goat's sweater to check her belly and udder. "The good news is, no coyote with a grain of sense would dare set foot on the property."

"Which is kinda pointless if he lets all the goats escape."

"Yeah, thinking we might need a backup, here," she said with an affectionate glance at the now-prone, sofa-size furball. "Not yet," she said, patting Begonia's back as she stood, then kneed her way through the small, bleating flock to inspect the grumpy-looking Jasmine. "Here, either. When their sides sink in, in front of their hips? That means labor's started."

"So you've done this before?"

"Oh, yeah. Just not with my own. What?"

"Nothing. Except...can't help but wonder why you bred 'em when you knew you'd be having a baby at the same time."

She almost laughed. "Nobody's ever accused me of being sane," she said, leaving the pen again. "But the whole point of starting the flock was to breed 'em for their fleece. And kid fleece is more valuable than older goats'. No babies, no point in keeping them. And Hunter and Zoey are so fired up about how cute the kids are gonna be..."

A faint blush colored her cheeks. "Sorry. Farming's not supposed to be about sentiment."

"Says who?"

"The people who actually make it work?"

Cash thought about that for a minute, then nodded toward the unfinished side of the house. "Kids said that was supposed to be a new room for Annie?"

"A studio and bedroom combo, yeah. And yes, it would've made more sense to build the addition and then rip out the wall. But Lee was so sure he'd be able to get it done before winter set in..." Her mouth pulled flat. "After the funeral, a couple of guys from church stuffed insulation between the studs and tacked up the plastic. Would've frozen for sure without it."

"Seems a shame. That you couldn't get it done."

She shrugged. "Life's like that sometimes."

Their gazes bumped into each other, hustled away.

"Well. Guess I'll go finish up in the greenhouse before it gets dark—"

"You know, I've got a big stew in the crockpot, huge, it'll take us a week to eat it all, you're welcome to have dinner with us—"

He frowned at her. "I thought I'd made my position clear on that."

"I know, but it doesn't feel right, you doing all this work without letting me repay you *some*how." Then she smiled. "I've been told I make a dynamite stew."

"I don't doubt it for a minute," Cash said quietly. "So thank you again. But no." Then he walked away, quickly, before he could change his mind. When he got to the greenhouse, however, he glanced back to see Emma, aglow in the afternoon sun, watching him with an expression he couldn't read.

And God only knew, didn't want to.

"What's wrong?" Emma puffed out as she lay like an up-ended beetle on her bed while the midwife, a stick figure in a wrinkled tee and baggy, drawstring pants, poked and prodded her beach-ball belly.

"Nothing's *wrong*." Patrice straightened, palming her buzz cut for a moment before motioning her assistant, Jewel, over for, Emma was guessing, a second opinion. While Patrice stood by, all jutting elbows and serious expression, the younger, ponytailed woman carefully palpated Emma's bare belly, then pushed her tiny, black-framed glasses up on her cute little nose. Frowning. "Um…it sure feels like the baby's breech."

"Oh, crud," Emma said, her head flopping back on her pillow.

"Nothing to get your panties in a wad about," Patrice said, dumping her stethoscope in her bag. "Since he's not engaged, he may well turn yet. I've got an incline board out in the truck, you can lie on that with your hips up for a half hour several times a day and let's see if that works."

"For heaven's sake, Patty," Emma began, but her breath got cut off when she tried to sit up. Inside, she was flailing, but outside it felt like she had cement blocks glued to her limbs.

With a little "Oh!" Jewel fluttered over. "Here, let me help you," she said as she tried to slip one slight arm behind Emma's shoulders. *Yeah, good luck with that,* Emma thought as she waved Miss Sunshine and Rainbows away and hauled herself upright on her own steam. Jewel's smile wilted slightly, only to perk right back up when Emma briefly squeezed her hand. The girl more than lived up to her name, but honestly—it was like trying to breathe in a cloud of cotton candy. Frankly, she preferred Patrice's pull-no-punches approach. Even if it was news she didn't want to hear.

"Like I've got time to lounge around with my hips up. In case you haven't noticed, I've got six goats about to kid. And crops to plant, and—"

"And you know I won't attempt a breech birth at home. So that kinda narrows your options. I'm sorry," Patrice said, not unkindly. For her. "It probably wouldn't hurt to talk to Naomi. As a backup," she added when Emma pouted.

Not that she had anything against their GP, but she'd loved birthing Zoey at home and had been seriously looking forward to another crack at it.

"Otherwise," Patrice was saying, "you're both doing great. Although you might want to keep an eye on those ankles, make sure they don't get any puffier."

"Heh. If I had a periscope, maybe."

"Okay, have somebody else keep an eye on 'em for you. Like Zoey." The midwife zipped up her case and started for the door. "You got anybody to get the incline board out of the truck?"

"Oh!" Jewel said, like a retriever told to fetch. "I'll go ask the guy we saw plowing when we drove up, how's that?"

And off she went, butt twitching and ponytail bobbing, before Emma could say, "Uh…"

Not that there was much choice, Emma thought as she and Patrice stood on her porch amidst milling cats and a comatose dog, watching Cash from atop the ancient John Deere frown down on the very animated Jewel. Kinda like a bulldog being accosted by a hyperfriendly toy poodle.

"Holy mother-of-pearl," Patrice breathed out. "Is that who I think it is?"

"Depends on who you think it is," Emma said.

"What in the hell is Cash Cochran doing back here?"

Nodding, but unsmiling, Cash dismounted from the Deere with the same graceful deliberateness he did everything. "Facing down demons, apparently."

"In your onion field?"

"Not sure you can pick and choose where your demons show up."

Although apparently he still wasn't ready to confront the ones in the house. Or maybe it was her he was avoiding, she couldn't quite tell. He'd even taken to bringing his own lunch to avoid any conversation outside of discussing the day's to-do list in the morning. Didn't even come inside to use the facilities, preferring—Emma assumed—the bare-bones john and sink in the greenhouse.

But Lordamercy, judging from the amount of work he'd done, he sure as heck was exorcising something. Trees pruned, fields plowed, new raised beds built, the leaking greenhouse repaired…the man was a miracle.

An enigma, but a miracle.

"You know him?" Emma asked the midwife.

"Personally? No. He'd've still been a kid when I left. Grew up somewhere around here, as I recall."

"Not somewhere around here. Right here. In this house."

"You're kidding?"

"Nope."

"Well, I'll be." Patrice paused. "I gather he had it pretty hard."

Funny thing about small-town gossip, the way everybody seemed to know part of a story but hardly anybody knew the whole thing. Especially people like Patrice, who'd been away most of her adult life, returning to Tierra Rosa only a few years ago.

"Lee and Cash were friends when they were kids," Emma said, watching Cash as he approached, the picture of forbearance as Jewel jabbered on at his side. "Although they'd…lost touch after Cash left. Guess he decided it was time to catch up."

"Hell," Patrice said.

"Yeah."

The midwife shielded her eyes. "He as good-looking as I think, or is that a trick of the light?"

If only. Not that he'd been exactly sickly looking when he'd first arrived, but a week's worth of manual labor in the strong New Mexico sun had already toasted his skin, more sharply defined muscles clearly visible underneath the T-shirts he'd taken to wearing once the temperature finally began to rise. Emma had never been one to drool over six-packs and taut abs and such—obviously—but even she had to admit the occasional glimpse of eye candy, even from a distance, handily distracted her from the last-month-of-pregnancy doldrums.

"Nope, not the light."

Patrice snorted. "He's almost enough to make me forget men don't do it for me."

"I take it you'd prefer I not mention that to Lucy."

"I'd appreciate it, yeah."

Wordlessly, Cash hauled the board out of Patrice's truck and up the steps. Bumble lifted his head, yawned, and thunked it back down again. "Where you want it?"

"Um…at the foot of the bed, I suppose."

Effortlessly shifting the board to angle it through the door, Cash carted it into the house. But not before his gaze glanced off Emma's, startling against his darkened skin and frustrating in its opacity.

The midwives took off and Emma freely expelled her sigh. Not that she knew, really, what the sigh was about, other than a general itchiness about things being not quite right. With Cash, about Cash, between Cash and her.

When he returned, Emma muttered her thanks, fully expecting one of his cursory nods before he stomped back to work. In fact, after an equally muttered, "No problem," he did head down the steps, only to turn back when he reached the bottom, his brows pulled together.

"What's that contraption for, anyway?"

With that, her more immediate worry hopscotched to the front of her brain. "The baby's in the wrong position. If he doesn't turn I probably won't be able to have him at home. So the slant board is for me to lie on with my hips up to encourage him to get with the program."

"Not a skateboard ramp, then."

Emma laughed. "Uh, no. Got on a skateboard exactly once. In college. Broke one wrist and sprained the other. Thus ended my extreme-sport career."

He didn't smile. "Does it work? Lying upside down?"

"Sometimes."

Disapproval heavy in his eyes, Cash yanked off his hat, slicking his forearm across his brow before clamping the hat back on. "Why on earth would you want to have the baby out here in the middle of nowhere, anyway, instead of in a hospital?"

Whoa. Not what she expected. "Sorry, but I'm not sure how that's any of your business."

"It's my business because Lee—"

He looked away, his jaw tight. Emma frowned. "Lee, what?"

A couple of beats passed before Cash looked up. "I haven't been entirely honest with you. About why I'm here. And I've been keeping out of your way more'n usual until I figured out whether I should say something or not."

Apprehension fisted in Emma's chest. "About what?"

Another moment sailed by before Cash said, "When Lee wrote to me, when y'all got the house, he asked…he asked me to look out for you and the kids if anything happened to him."

She nearly lost her breath. "You're not serious."

"I'll even show you the letter, if you want."

Her knees giving way, Emma awkwardly lowered herself to the porch step, nearly taking out a cat in the process. Bumble roused himself to come make it better. She pushed him away. "Lee wouldn't tell you about your father, but he—" Pressing her fingertips into the space between her brows, she squeezed shut her eyes. Opened them again. "And you agreed?"

"Not exactly," Cash said with a strained slant to his mouth. "But I didn't say no, either. I just never thought…you know."

"No. No, of course not." Feeling slightly dizzy, Emma leaned against the porch stair railing. "So that's why you're here? Doing all this? Because Lee asked you as a favor to him a million years ago?"

"More or less. Yeah."

Even as the words left his lips, though, she caught the that's-my-story-and-I'm-sticking-to-it look in his eyes. So. He was only here out of a sense of duty, then. Of obligation. And yet…

And yet, Cash had never actually *promised* to fulfill the favor Lee had asked of him. Meaning that, in reality, there was no obligation. Except, apparently, in Cash's head.

Forget enigma. The man was flat-out bizarre.

"Well. Thank you. Again. But I somehow doubt Lee meant 'looking out for' to include butting in about how and where I give birth."

"And maybe I think it does. I mean…what would Lee want?"

They glared at each other for a moment or two before the absurdity of the whole situation set a laugh to tickling deep inside Emma's chest, before, a split second later, it erupted in a loud screech.

"I'm serious," Cash said, clearly offended.

"Oh, honey, I know you a-are." She swallowed, fighting for control. "And I appreciate your concern, I really do. But since Lee was completely on board with a home birth for Zoey, I don't think he'd be terribly wigged out about it this time. Anyway, since Lee's not here, the issue is…moot."

When she struggled to stand again, Cash lunged forward to grab her hand, his own strong and rough and warm, and again she was struck by how he seemed to take up far more space than his body warranted. How that raw animal magnetism seemed at such odds with the sense of unworthiness vibrating at its core.

He just needs somebody to love him. Like Charlie Brown's Christmas tree.

Cash let go and stepped back, like he'd read her mind, and it hit her that something more than simple obligation was definitely at work here. Something confusing the heck out of him.

But pointing out what was so clear to her would only embarrass him, she was sure. If not fall on deaf ears altogether. Because she doubted Cash was ready to believe in his own goodness any more than he did the Tooth Fairy. Not that this was her problem.

Problem, no. Opportunity, yes.

One day she was gonna have serious words with that chick in her head.

For now, though, she said, "There's something you need to understand, Cash. Sure, Lee and I made all the major decisions about the kids, our life, together. But we also trusted each other to do whatever we thought was best when the other one wasn't around. And right before he died…"

Emma glanced down, taking a careful, deep breath before looking at Cash again. "He said he'd come back and haunt me if I made any decisions out of some misguided sense of honoring his memory. Or from fear of what other people might think. So I'm guessing Lee would want you to trust me, too. After all, you were the one who said we shouldn't get tangled up in each other's lives, right?"

Never mind that she was already getting more and more tangled, simply because she couldn't pull off *detached* if her life depended on it. Any more than Lee did. But Cash didn't have to know that.

After a moment, he nodded. But he didn't look real convinced.

Men, honestly, Emma thought, then said, "If it makes you feel better, Patrice has been doing this for twenty years. The woman knows her stuff. I swear, taking unnecessary chances isn't her thing. Any more than it is mine. I had Hunter in the hospital," she said before Cash could protest again, "because we knew he was a Down's baby and might need extra attention after he was born. But Zoey was a low-risk pregnancy, so we had her at home. Good thing, too, since I would've never made it to the hospital, she came so fast." She shrugged. "It'd be great to do it again, but if it doesn't work out…I'll deal."

His eyes grazed hers. "Like you do with everything else."

"Exactly."

Bumble stretched, yawned, glanced over at the goats to make sure everything was okey-dokey, then padded down to Cash for a head scratch. He obliged, then said, "Looks like the weather should hold long enough to get those two fields planted in the next couple days, if that's okay with you."

But he was gone before she could answer, trudging across the yard like the whole world was sitting on his shoulders. With a sigh, Emma went back inside.

"What the hell is this thing?" Annie called from Emma's bedroom.

"Baby's breech," Emma said when she eventually made it down the hall. "I'm supposed to lie upside down to encourage him to turn around."

"Then you best get to it."

"Can't. Got dinner to start—"

"And the day I can't stick a chicken in the oven you can go ahead and shoot me. Oh, by the way—" this said with a smack to Emma's arm "—I'm all out of white acrylic. And canvases. And it looks like we're running low on dog food. Cat food, too. In fact, have you even looked at the pantry recently? Gettin' kinda bare in there. So next time you go into Santa Fe, let me know, I'll give you a list."

Then she pointed one steady, take-no-prisoners hand at the board. *"Now,"* she said, and Emma released a long, surrendering breath and awkwardly lowered herself onto the board, where it occurred to her that *upside down* pretty much described her entire life these days.

Chapter Five

As the setting sun rippled across the fields in jagged orange stripes, Cash opened his car door the precise moment Emma flagged him down, a bulging plastic grocery bag knocking against her thigh as she marched out to him.

He steeled himself. Not because of whatever she wanted to say, but because the woman was seriously messing with his head. Her busting out laughing like that earlier, for instance… he bet she had no idea how contagious it was.

Or how much he'd wanted to crawl inside that laugh, pull it around him like a thick, soft sleeping bag.

Not good.

"Got a favor to ask," she said as she neared, her hair so bright from the sun he could barely look at it. The dog followed her, a giant, four-footed, peach-colored marshmallow.

"Oh?"

"I know you were fixing to get the peppers and beans in tomorrow, but I was wondering if you could take me and the kids into Santa Fe instead?" She shielded her eyes from the sun. "I've got a list a mile long for Sam's Club and I don't think I should be hauling around bags of dog food that weigh more than the kids do. Normally I'd ask one of my girlfriends, but everybody's busy. We can take the Suburban," she said, nodding in the direction of the rhinoceros-like relic, parked next to the muddiest, most beat-up pickup north of Albuquerque. Cash stared at the car, his brain frozen. "'Course, if you'd rather we go in your car, that'd be okay, too."

"No, it's not that, it's…"

Yeah. Can't wait to hear how you're gonna finish that sentence.

"I promise, I'll keep quiet, if you want," she said, a smile flirting with her mouth when he faced her again. "But you're on your own with the kids. Unfortunately they don't come with off buttons—"

"We can take whatever car you like," he said, thinking this would be a helluva lot easier if Lee'd married somebody mean. Or stupid. Or ugly. "When you wanna go?"

"Early, before it gets crowded. I wouldn't normally have the kids, but they're off from school and I don't like leaving 'em alone for that long. And Annie's got her art class at nine. So we can drop her on the way. Here." She handed over the bag. "It's the last of the stew, the troops have threatened flat-out insurrection if I pawn it off on 'em one more time."

The bottom of the bag was warm, the rich fragrance teasing even through the tightly closed plastic container inside.

"Green chile?"

"You bet. Wouldn't feel like New Mexico otherwise. Enjoy," she said, then turned and walked away, her wide hips swaying to balance the load in front as the dog trotted along beside her.

Don't look. Don't think. Just…don't.

By the time Cash got back to his house, he couldn't get the lid off fast enough. He dimly remembered his mother saying how the last of the stew was always the best, and it was certainly true here—you could hardly see the large, tender chunks of beef, the onion-and-chile-saturated potatoes, in the thick sauce. He settled into the leather sectional that'd come with the place and dug in, frowning slightly at the still-unpacked boxes lining the far wall. By rights he should've hauled 'em into the garage by now, since they'd probably never get unpacked.

Sighing, Cash set the half-empty container on the end table and melted into the sofa cushions, his hands laced behind his head as he stared at the boxes. And beyond them, the custom-made plank table in the dining room he never used. Would never use, more'n likely.

What the hell was he doing here?

On another heavy breath, he propelled himself off the sofa and down the hall, to the room he'd set up as his music studio. God knew why, since he'd had no desire to even pick up a guitar since he'd come back. For years, he'd been inseparable from his music. But now…

He banged his palm on the doorjamb and returned to the living room, his scratched-up, blistered hands buried in his front pockets. Limbo, that was where he was, caught between a life that no longer worked and one that didn't even exist.

Who the hell was he?

His reaction to Emma's wanting a home birth had damn near knocked him for a loop. That it mattered. That he cared about something that, like she said, was none of his business. And yet, looking at her belly, catching glimpses of her kids laughing and fooling around, it was hard not to feel like he'd missed out on the only real worthwhile thing there was—

Yet another road he knew better than to go down. But, man, those entrance ramps sure did sneak up on a person.

Expelling a humorless chuckle, Cash plucked the container off the end table, spooning in the last few bites of now-cold stew, telling himself the sooner Emma had this baby and he could leave, the better. Except...

Except what the hell was he supposed to do then?

The silence rang in his ears.

Wasn't even eight-thirty when Cash showed up, apparently ready to get this little field trip over with.

"So. Your car—" this said with a derisive glance toward her banged-up Suburban "—or mine?"

Ignoring the dull ache in her lower back, Emma gave him a smile. "And good morning to you, too," she said, then called back into the house, "Annie! Kids! Let's go." Then she faced Cash again. "Yours is fine. Especially since I don't much feel like driving."

He immediately frowned. "You sure you should go?"

"Yep, unless you want to take the kids to Sam's on your own."

They barreled past them. Screaming. "How hard could it be?"

"You don't want to know. Annie! For pity's sake—!"

"I'm coming, I'm coming, keep your shirt on!" Cheerfully attired in a bilious lavender exercise suit and a wide-brimmed straw hat with scarf ties, Annie finally appeared in the doorway, struggling to keep cats inside while hanging onto her paint box and tabletop easel. "These bones don't exactly move at the speed of light, you know. Hello, Cash. You're looking fit this morning. You're also looking...different. Lordamercy, what happened to your hair?"

Emma's head snapped back around. Yes, she'd officially reached the stage where the pregnancy was pushing against her eyeballs, because she'd totally missed that little detail. She didn't miss, however, Cash's almost-sheepish smile when he lifted his hand, skimming his free hand over the skull-hugging haircut that made his eyes glow like polished silver coins in his darkened face and brought every bone in that face into sharp relief. "Like it?"

"Hell, yes," Annie said, finally shutting the door and nearly dropping her paint box in the process.

"Here, let me get those," Cash said, taking the box and easel from her and carting them out to his car.

"Say what you will," Annie whispered. Sort of. "He's a polite young man."

Uh-huh.

"Not to mention hot."

Yeah. That, too. Could life *get* any more unfair?

To save wear and tear on her nerves, Emma sat in the very back until they'd dropped Annie off at her art class, by which time the old woman had talked the poor man's ears off. Although about what Emma couldn't say, since the kids' excited chattering between them gobbled up Annie's conversation.

Annie settled, Emma hoisted her pregnant self into the passenger seat, almost immediately wishing she hadn't. Although her sense of smell had dimmed a bit from first-trimester-bloodhound stage, it was still up there. Enough that Cash's shower-fresh scent sparked a not-so-tiny urge to take a bite out of the man's neck.

"What's so funny?" he asked when she giggled.

"Um, nothing." She giggled again, only to wince when Junior clobbered her one.

"You look different, too," Cash said, sparing her a brief glance as they pulled out onto the highway to take them to Santa Fe. "But I can't figure out how."

"That would be makeup." She batted her eyes. "Because trips to Sam's Club bring out the girly-girl in me."

He almost smiled. Maybe. Hard to tell. Then he leaned forward to punch on the radio, only to punch it right off when one of his own recordings came on. Emma didn't think she'd ever seen a man blush so hard. Especially when her darling son said behind her, "That was you! On the ra-dio! Put it on again! Please? I real-ly like that one."

Looking like he wanted to vanish into thin air, Cash slowly turned the radio back on. Only to laugh—God bless him— when Hunter and Zoey both started singing along. At the tops of their lungs.

"At least I don't have to hear myself this way," he shouted over the caterwauling in the backseat.

Finally the song ended, followed by Martina McBride, who the kids apparently didn't want to do the karaoke thing with. Thank God for small blessings.

"Mr. Coch-ran?"

"Yeah, Hunter?"

"Can you teach me to play the gui-tar?"

"Hunter, for heaven's sake—!"

"Sure. Why not?"

Emma gawked at Cash, then frowned out the window until the noise level behind them rose sufficiently for her to speak undetected. "Please don't patronize him, Cash."

At his silence, she dared to look over. His jaw was working overtime. "God knows I've got my faults, but patronizing a kid isn't one of 'em." Another chilly glance preceded, "If I said I'll teach him, I'll teach him."

Facing front again, she said, "He's…he's not exactly a fast learner."

"Then it's lucky for him I wasn't, either."

Heat scorched Emma's cheeks. "Sorry. I'm just…"

"Looking out for your kid. I get it. Maybe I didn't exactly have a lot of firsthand experience with the concept, but I do recognize it when I see it." His gaze flicked her way, then back out the windshield. "You'd be surprised how many songs you can fake with only three chords," he said, more gently. "Judging from how careful Hunter is with his chores, I imagine he'll do fine."

"You've seen him do his chores?"

"Occasionally, yeah."

Emma drummed her fingers on her knee. "Where do you plan on giving him these lessons?"

He paused. "In the house. If that's okay with you."

"Me? Yes." She glanced over. "But you—"

"It's just a house. And *your* house, to boot. Like you said—nothing in there to hurt me anymore."

For a moment or two, Emma stared at Cash's hand on the steering wheel, the graceful curve of his strong fingers, before letting her gaze scuttle away as she contemplated the man so sure he wasn't a good person.

The seat belt was about to strangle her; she tried to adjust it, gave up. "What I said before, about being sick to death of Lee talking about you all the time? That didn't mean there weren't times when one of your songs would get me to crying like a baby."

"No need to butter me up," he said after a moment. "You'll still get your fields planted."

Emma laughed. "I'm not that conniving. But it's true. I mean, I haven't got a molecule of musical talent, but what you have…it comes from the heart. I can see why you made it big."

After a long pause, he said, "Thank you. But whatever you think you hear or see…" His eyes cut to hers. "It's called *performing*, Emma. Making the illusion seem real." He returned his gaze to the road. "I have no idea, to be honest, where it comes from, but it's not my heart. Gotta have one of those for that to happen."

Honestly. If he hadn't've been driving, she would've smacked him upside the head for sure. Instead, she said, "You miss it?"

Another several seconds' silence preceded, "At the moment? Not really."

She couldn't decide whether to believe him or not.

When they got to Sam's after picking up Annie's supplies at Hobby Lobby, the kids clambered onto one of the flatbeds, begging Cash to push. Emma headed toward the pet food section, which seemed to take a lot longer to get to than during her last trip here. Behind her, kids yakked away to Cash over the flatbed's rumbling and rattling, the occasional *beep beep beep* of a forklift gliding down an aisle of the megawarehouse store.

"Two of those, two of those and three cases of that," she said when they stopped, after which Cash toted those fifty-pound bags like they were nothin' and Emma ogled. Cheap thrills and all that. Amazingly, not one soul recognized him. Or at least not that she could tell. Even with the hair gone bye-bye, she would've expected at least one fan to pop up out of the woodwork—or steel shelving, in this case—and ask for his autograph. Weird.

'Course, he'd been dead silent since they'd gotten inside, too. Minute he opened his mouth, though, the jig would be up. Unfortunately, the longer he stayed mute, the more uneasy Emma got. So as soon as the kids scrambled off their erstwhile amusement-park ride to run up and down the empty aisle, she apologized. While pointing to a jumbo box of toilet paper. Forty-eight rolls. Twenty-four of which, alas, she'd use all by herself within the week.

Cash thunked the toilet paper onto the flatbed, then looked at her like she was nuts. "Apologize for what?"

Compared with not looking at her at all, she counted that as a step up. She pointed again and a twelve-roll package of paper towels thumped alongside the toilet paper.

"Even for you, you've been quiet. So it finally dawned on me that maybe being out in public makes you uncomfortable."

One hand on the flatbed handle, he shoved the other into his front pocket. Sexiest pose ever. "In case you missed it, I'm not much for talking if I don't have anything to say. Don't take it personal. But I'm not uncomfortable at all. In fact…" His gaze swung to the kids, who, what with all their hooting and hollering, might've embarrassed her if she hadn't been so darn pregnant. "It feels good, doing something ordinary. Something normal." One side of his mouth lifted. "Kind of a novel experience, you know?"

And right then she saw why nobody recognized him: because this man was nothing like the star people couldn't take their eyes off. This man was at peace. At peace for Cash, anyway. And real. The man on the videos, in the tabloids, was like that fake marble stuff in her one bathroom—it was okay as long as you didn't look too hard. Or expect it be something it wasn't.

He was absolutely right, about the illusion thing. Although Emma had never seen him wear anything other than jeans or baggy carpenter pants and a T-shirt when he performed, now it hit her that, when he was on stage he wore a costume every bit as much as Elvis had. For all his fans thought he connected with them, all they'd actually gotten was the Cash he'd pretended to be until the real one showed up.

Although probably nobody, least of all him, would've expected that to be in the paper goods aisle in Sam's Club.

"You know," he said, watching the kids, "I would've given my eyeteeth for the chance to run around like that. To not feel judged all the time."

The longing in his voice, his eyes, clogged her throat. "We do—did—our best to find the balance between freedom and good manners. Although to be fair this is a little more freedom than they're usually given in a public place. Any moment, somebody's bound to tell 'em to hush."

Turned out she didn't have to, since the kids ran up, laughing and out of breath. Zoey collapsed on the flatbed with a great, dramatic sigh. "Are we done yet? I'm *starving!*"

"Yeah. Me, too," Hunter put in. "C'n I get a hot dog and piz-za?"

"You cannot. One or the other, that's the deal."

"But last time we were here *you* got both."

"That's because one was for the baby." Out of the corner of her eye, she caught Cash's smile, and she thought, *Yes. Like that.*

Hunter crossed his arms, scowling. He was usually pretty laid-back, but when his stubborn streak kicked in, watch out. "Not fair."

Emma leaned over to cup her son's smooth hair, kiss his forehead. A move that would've gotten her a distressed, "Mo-om!" from any other twelve-year-old boy.

"Tell you what—you can both get churros, too."

"Yeah!" Hunter said, pumping his fist as Zoey nodded so hard her curls blurred.

Crisis #9756 averted, Emma thought wearily, directing the flatbed captain to shore while she trudged along beside, thinking a drive-through baby-delivery service sounded good, right about now.

Then, as she dug in her wallet for her credit card after going through the line, Cash stepped in front of her to swipe his card through the little doohickey, and her brain shorted out.

"For heaven's sake," she said, shoving him aside to swipe her own. "I didn't ask you along so you'd pay for me."

"No, if I recall you asked me to come along to help you with the heavy sh—stuff. Picking up the tab was my idea."

"Well, forget it," she said, flashing a tight nothing-to-see-here-move-along smile for the cashier as she took her membership card and receipt. Even so, tension vibrated between them as Cash navigated the flatbed toward the food counter. When the kids scampered ahead to get in line, she said in a low voice, "Maybe I've got a few more bills than I'd like right now, but we're not destitute."

Exactly.

"Didn't think you were." He parked the flatbed alongside the row of tables. Leaned on the handle. Lasered her with those eyes. Yeah, she was definitely seeing some quality time with her Bible and the Good Lord in her near future.

"Then why did you—?"

"Because it felt right. Nothin' more to it than that. Oh, and by the way…I already slipped Zoey a twenty to pay for lunch."

"When on earth did you—?"

"Doing things behind people's backs is one of my many talents."

"Is that a warning?"

Cash's forehead scrunched, like he was thinking it over, then nodded. "That's probably your safest bet, yeah. You also might want to think about getting yourself on up there," he said, with another nod toward the counter, "before they spend it all on themselves. And get me a pizza slice and a Coke while you're at it," he yelled toward her back as she waddled off, thinking things were a lot easier when he *didn't* talk to her.

By the time Cash delivered Emma and the kids back to the house, it'd started to rain. Then he volunteered to fetch Annie from her art class, since Emma was obviously pooped. Those big eyes of hers practically glowed with gratitude. He'd have to watch out for that. In any case, what with the rain and the fetching and everything, the planting got put on hold for another day or so.

Good thing, considering how Emma'd looked at him in the store, like she could see straight through all the cobwebs into that dark, dank place he called his brain.

Because first off, he sincerely doubted she saw whatever she thought she saw in there. Shadows, was all there were, constantly shifting, insubstantial as dust. Second, he didn't need some woman going all pitying and "I can fix that" on him. Pity, he didn't want or need. And after all this time it was pretty obvious he wasn't fixable.

So what in tarnation compelled him, once he'd left the farm, to check the town's lone hock shop on the off-chance that they had a three-quarter acoustic guitar, he had no idea. Sure, he could buy new, but he figured Emma was less likely to go all indignant on him if he gave Hunter one that was a little banged up.

As it happened, the sunken-cheeked, ponytailed dude behind the counter had exactly what Cash was looking for. Even came with a case and a packet of new strings. Back in his truck, Cash watched the rain slither down the windshield, trying to identify the strange, tickly sensation in his chest. Eventually he decided this must be what it felt like to do something right.

Kinda like the first time he had Greek food. Sorta weird, but not so bad once he got used to it.

Then he got another idea, brought on by Annie's worry about how well the plastic sheeting on the side of the house would hold up in the rain. One that sent him to Ortega's, a kick-ass Mexican diner in town that'd been around for probably two decades before Cash'd been born and was, according to Emma, the local answer to Google—whatever you were looking for or needed to know, you were sure to find it, or find it out, there.

Shaking water off his hat, Cash slipped inside, nodding at the dark-haired, heavyset woman behind the cash register.

"Hey, Evangelista!" somebody called out. "What's the holdup with my *huevos,* babydoll? I'm starving over here!"

"Keep your shirt on, Teo, Jose's makin' 'em up special, jus' for you. And who you calling babydoll?" she added, getting a toothless cackle in response. Shaking her head, she duck-walked over to Cash's table, past the harried little waitress unloading six people's orders at the corner booth. "What can I get for you, handsome?" she said, bosoms swaying as she took a rag to his table. "Jus' took cheese enchiladas out of the oven, how's that?"

"Just coffee for now. Although…maybe you could help me. I recently moved into a house up on Coyote Trail, but I don't remember the name of the guy who did the remodel—"

"Madre de Dios." Evangelista straightened, one hand on her wide hip. "You're Cash Cochran?"

"Yeah."

"Chrissy!" she barked. "Get me a cup of coffee over here! Now!" Then she turned back to Cash, stars twinkling in her flat, dark eyes. "You sure you don' want some of those enchiladas? They're on the house—"

Cash smiled. "No, no, coffee's fine. Thanks."

The young, blandly pretty waitress hustled over with the coffee, recognized him and gasped, then scurried off, looking back over her shoulder like she couldn't believe what she'd seen.

"Guy you're looking for is Eli Garrett," Evangelista said as Cash took a sip of the strong, black coffee, ignoring the stares and whispers. And shrugs. Spotty fan base up here, would be his guess. "Him and his brothers and father, they got a woodworking shop about a mile that way." She nodded north.

"Eli, right. He made some of the furniture in the house. Real talented."

"Whole family's like that. Although Noah's who you want now, he's taken over the construction end of the business so Eli can keep on with his furniture making. Big sign out front, says Garrett's Woodworking, you can't miss it. You wan' that coffee to go?" she said when he rose.

"Please." When she returned with fresh coffee in a foam cup, Cash said, "You guys deliver?"

"Up to your place? Sure—"

"No, not for me. To my old…to the Manning farm, east of town?"

"Yeah, I know where that is."

He pulled out a pair of twenties. "Why don't you send a tray of those enchiladas on up there whenever you get the chance? And maybe a couple of sides to go with them? Will this cover it?"

"Easily," she said, taking the money. "Let me get you your change—"

"Not necessary," he said, taking his coffee and walking out, pulling his jacket collar up against the now-pelting rain as he contemplated that what he was about to do would either make him look like a hero for the first time in his life, or a total jackass.

Which wouldn't be anything new at all.

Chapter Six

Rubbing her belly, Emma stared blearily out the front window at the soggy gray morning. Generally speaking, she loved the rain. Like anybody else who lived in the Southwest—particularly anybody insane enough to try farming in the Southwest—she welcomed it, worshipped it, sang its praises and collected every drop she could in a dozen rain barrels set up around the house. Rain was a blessing.

By the second day of nonstop blessedness, however, she'd pretty much had it—with the mud, the stir-crazy kids, the damp seeping in through the unfinished side of the house, her inability to get anything done that needed doing. Her stinky dog. If it didn't stop soon, she was in sore danger of becoming cranky.

And that would be unacceptable.

Puffy feet rammed into Lee's ugly-as-sin boots, a plastic poncho floating around her whale-esque body, she and her disgusting dog slogged through the wet and the goop to the barn to check on the goats, none of whom looked any happier than she did. Hunter had changed out the straw yesterday, but it was already gross, so she changed it again. The goats seemed grateful. Miserable, but grateful.

The mamas fed and fussed over, she trudged over to the greenhouse to check on her hothouse lettuces, cukes and tomatoes, only to nearly have a heart attack when she turned to find a grim-faced Cash standing in the doorway, water dripping off his hat brim.

"For future reference?" she said, her voice raised over the deluge on the plastic roof. "It's not generally a good idea to sneak up on a pregnant woman."

"I wasn't sneaking. I called out when you left the barn, but you couldn't hear me."

Emma scraped aside a splat of hair plastered against her cheek, thinking it was pathetic how good the man looked soaking wet. Even more pathetic, though, was that all it took to turn her head these days was a surprise delivery of enchiladas, refried beans and Spanish rice. And sopapillas, which would've done the trick all by themselves.

She'd called to thank him when they'd arrived, of course, but she felt honor-bound to mention it again. "I got two full meals off those enchiladas, by the way."

"Glad to hear it. They were okay, then?"

"You kidding? Evangelista rocks. You should try her tamales sometime. Guaranteed to cure what ails you."

At the puzzled look in Cash's eyes, she grabbed a tray to collect the cherry tomatoes, her poncho crinkling like cellophane. "Didn't expect you today."

"Why not?"

"Unless somebody gives birth, not much going on."

"Don't notice you lying around with your feet up. Which you probably *should* be doing."

Emma smirked. "It was get out of that house or lose my mind. Can't stand being cooped up. Besides, these puppies can't wait. When they're ready, they're ready."

"Need help?"

"Knock yourself out."

Glancing over, she caught his half smile and got all warm and fizzy inside, which was wrong on *so* many levels. *There you go, being nice again,* she wanted to say. But didn't. Cash grabbed another tray and started carefully plucking tomatoes across from her, only to suddenly look up. Frowning.

"Why does it sound like a highfalutin restaurant in here?"

"You came in at the classical part of the loop. But they like soft jazz, ragtime and Big Band, too."

"They?"

"The vegetables. The goats, too, as it happens. Except the speaker's broken in the barn."

"You're putting me on."

"No, the speaker's really broken—"

"About *lettuce* liking music."

"What can I tell you? We get something like twice the yield with music playing than we do if it's silent." She met his incredulous gaze. Held up her hand. "Crazy earth mother chick, here. Although I draw the line at crystals."

Cash actually laughed, then scanned the three rows of two-foot-tall raised beds, teeming with veggies in various stages. "You sell all this stuff?"

"Most of it. Local restaurants, the farmers' market. Sometimes a roadside stand when the weather's good. My church gets whatever doesn't sell to give to whoever needs it. Obviously we do more during the summer, but this definitely keeps us going the rest of the year. That, and our canned goods. I usually make delivery runs two, three times a week."

"Busy lady."

"Name me a farmer who isn't."

"Whose idea was the raised beds?"

"Lee's," she said, straightening to ease her aching back. Realizing she no longer imagined seeing her husband out of the corner of her eye, giving pep talks to the peppers. "Took him most of that first winter to build them. But this way we can control the soil and irrigation much better than in-the-ground planting. And plant crops closer together. Small-farm agriculture was his emphasis at New Mexico State. That's where we met."

"I wondered. What'd you major in?"

"Animal husbandry. Always thought I'd have a ranch, someday. Like my folks did. In Texas."

"Did?"

"Mama and Daddy sold the ranch proper when Daddy started showing symptoms of Alzheimer's a few years ago. Nothing left but the house and garden now."

"I'm sorry." Emma shrugged. "Your daddy, is he…?"

"Still hanging in there. I keep trying to get Mama to get in some help so she could get a break every now and then. But all she says is, what if he has a lucid moment and she's not there?" Tears threatened; she blinked them back. "We talk several times a week, but we hardly see each other anymore. I can't leave here, and she won't leave him. She won't even be able to come see the baby after he's born."

"Damn," Cash said gently. "You've had it rough."

Emma knew if she looked up, saw the compassion she heard in his voice, she'd lose it for sure. "Taking the bad with the good," she said, yanking tomatoes off their vines, "that's just life. But the challenges…" At last she met his gaze. "The challenges make you dig deeper, to listen harder for the good in the midst of the bad. Because that's what gets you through."

* * *

Not for the first time, Cash felt chastened by Emma's soul-deep belief in whatever it was that kept her going, kept her from acting the martyr. Her courage. Her grace.

Her unfeigned goodness.

Because there was a difference between doing the occasional good deed and *being* good. Not that he could define it, exactly, but he sure as hell knew he fell into the first category, while Emma stood firmly in the second.

"Your folks...they had goats?" he said, changing the subject.

"A few," she said with a quick glance in his direction. In the humid greenhouse, curls sprouted around her face, little wispy things that made her look a lot younger than her mid-thirties. "To go with the sheep. They also had llamas, ostriches and a zebra or two."

"That's not a ranch, it's a zoo."

She laughed. Man, he was gonna miss that laugh. "Daddy's dream was to someday turn the ranch into a wildlife refuge. That was as close as he got."

"What about you? You have the same dream?"

"Not even. I'll stick with goats, thank you. For now, anyway."

They harvested in silence for a few minutes, violin music weaving through the rain's relentless pummeling. Cash had to admit, the music was soothing. Maybe he'd add a string accompaniment to his next song.

The thought startled him. Although, when he'd picked up his own guitar this morning to bring it along with the one he'd bought for Hunter, his fingers had tingled...

"You keep increasing your herd," he said suddenly, making Emma's head snap up across from him, "you're gonna need more room."

"Tell me something I don't know." Moving down the row, she said, "Lee said this was originally several hundred acres?"

"What my father owned outright, yep. Did a lot of grazing on government land, too." Following Emma's lead, Cash set the full tray on a nearby shelf, grabbed another. There was also something soothing about picking vegetables, the calm repetitiveness of it, the cool feel of them in his hand, the smell of the earth. Being around a woman who, for a change, seemed content with who she was. What she had.

"I was still real little the first time I went with my brothers and father to move the cows closer to home before they calved. Maybe five? Nearly froze my butt off." A melancholy smile stretched his mouth. "Never had so much fun in my life."

"This was before things went south, then?"

Her directness somehow deflated what'd been so blown up in his mind all these years. Somewhat, anyway. "Yeah. But you know, even after the bad stuff started, long as we were working cattle, he was okay. Better, anyway. It was like…I can't explain it. Like all that space…it seemed to absorb the craziness, somehow. Or at least dilute it. Maybe that's why I love the sky so much. The openness." He hesitated, then said, "Nowhere else I went could even begin to compare."

"Then why not stay?"

Why her question threw him, Cash had no idea. It wasn't personal. Or even particularly prying. In fact, she wasn't even looking at him, her long fingers moving like lightning as she picked the little tomatoes. Then he realized, it wasn't the question bugging him. It was the answer.

"Because there's been too many changes," he said quietly. "I don't recognize anything anymore. Don't recognize myself. I guess I thought, if I came back, maybe I could…I don't know. Start over. Pick up the missing thread. Except strangely enough, nothing waited for me to do that."

Emma straightened, fisting her lower back as she frowned at him, like she was puzzling something out. "But does starting over mean taking up where you left off? Or being open to new beginnings? Seems to me life's all about going forward, don't you think?"

Damn the woman for being logical. Worse, for being right.

"I brought over a guitar for Hunter," he said, fresh heat surging up his neck as he looked away. "It's just a student acoustic, nothing fancy, but decent enough to learn on. I was lucky to find a three-quarter size, though—I noticed his arms are too short for a full-size—"

"You bought him a guitar?"

"Used. Cheap," he said, eyes pinned to hers, daring her to go there. She took the hint and didn't. "I figured," he continued, "since it was raining and I knew the kids were off school, today might be a good time to start his lessons."

Emma gave him one of those long, unsettling looks, then nodded. "I'm sure that'll be fine with him. On one condition."

"And what's that?"

"You let me feed you first."

"You're assuming I haven't eaten."

One brow lifted. "Have you?"

"Toast and coffee." His stomach growled. "Two hours ago." She laughed, and Cash grinned in spite of himself. "You don't give up easy, do you?"

"Would be a pretty lousy farmer if I did," she said, setting aside her tray and dusting off her hands. "Not to mention a mother. Now. Would you rather have French toast or pancakes with your bacon?"

If nothing else, Cash had always been clear about what he wanted. Always. Stay or run like hell, didn't matter as long as he knew which was the right choice. Now, for the first time in his life, both of those were screaming in his head with equal shrillness, that old survival instinct warring with a yearning the likes of which he hadn't encountered in more years than he could count.

"French toast, if it's not too much trouble," he said at last, earning him a grin that made him simultaneously feel on top of the world and like total slime.

At this rate, his head would explode before the week was out.

Zoey was still half-asleep—she felt all stuffy again, like she was getting another cold—when she heard the commotion from the living room. Propping herself up on one elbow, she sneezed, blew her nose, then bent her head. Sure enough, she heard Cash's low voice, then Mama's. Then Hunter's. What the heck?

The sneeze unblocked her nose enough to make her feel like getting up to see what was going on. Besides, she was hungry and it smelled like bacon. Which meant there'd probably be French toast or pancakes or maybe even waffles to go with it. Yay.

Nobody noticed her at first, but that was okay because she wasn't an attention hog, as Granny put it. In fact, Zoey hated being fussed over. Especially when people did it 'cause they felt sorry for her, which only made her feel creepy and uncomfortable instead of better. Why didn't people *get* that? Honest to Pete.

Anyway, Cash'd brought Hunter a guitar so he could learn how to play. Huddled inside her fuzzy sweatshirt—the rain had made it all cold again—Zoey grinned. Hunter had been wanting a guitar for forever. He loved music and was always singing, and now he could play, too. Zoey didn't feel the least bit jealous. Music wasn't her thing, anyway. She had her art.

What she did feel, though, between all the *scrumptious* cooking smells and Hunter's grin as he turned his new guitar over and over in his hands, and Mama, standing in the doorway to the kitchen looking actually *happy,* was like things were good again. Almost like they'd been before Daddy died.

Happiness fizzing up inside her, Zoey ran across the room to give Cash a big old hug. For a moment she couldn't tell if he was mad or just surprised. But then he smiled, too, and she knew everything was gonna be okay.

After breakfast, Annie banished Emma from the kitchen to do the cleaning up. When Emma protested, the old woman smacked her with a dish towel. "Hiding's for wimps," she said. "Now git."

So she got.

"Move, cat," she said, shooing the Other Gray One out of the only armchair in the tiny room to lower her bulk into it. Immediately Zoey brought over a footstool, giving her a stern look until Emma put her feet up. The fire in the woodstove lazily hissed and snapped, competing with the drum of rain on the now-repaired roof. Perched on the edge of the worn plaid sofa, Hunter quivered with excitement as he watched Cash tune his "new" guitar. At their feet, Zoey plopped down on her stomach, chin in hands, absolutely riveted, neither she nor Cash apparently any the worse for wear from her spontaneous show of affection earlier.

Never mind that Emma had nearly dropped the baby right then and there.

Now, lulled into a full-bellied, fire-warmed stupor, she sank farther into the old cushions, even as her eyes watered from missing her husband. Until, through the blur, she noticed the look of expectancy on her children's faces, the twinkle of what could only be called mischief in Cash's eyes.

"Okay, now," he said. "This song's real easy, it only needs three chords. First one's a G." He placed three fingers on the fret. "You see that?" Hunter nodded, then tried to mimic where Cash had placed his three fingers. "Hold on, guy, I'll show you in a minute. Just listen, okay?"

At Hunter's emphatic nod, Cash sang, pulling a funny face, switching chords from time to time. "On top of spa-*ghe*-tti, all covered in cheeeese…"

Both kids started to giggle.

"I lost my poor meat-ball, when somebody sneezed. It rolled off the *ta*-ble, and onto the floor…and then my poor meat-ball, rolled right out the door…"

Both kids dissolved into peals of laughter, and Emma's pregnancy hormones ran amok. Cash had the same off-the-wall sense of humor as Lee? Who knew?

The song was old as the hills, but for whatever reason neither of her kids had heard it. Kids who'd clearly inherited their father's propensity for wince-worthy jokes. Hunter took enormous pride in knowing every knock-knock joke ever created, the vast majority of which he'd gotten from his father.

Remembering all the times Lee used to make her laugh hard enough to wet her pants, she suddenly understood how this man and her husband could have been best friends. Beyond the outcasts-bonding-together thing, that was.

They were both nuttier than fruitcakes.

Still, was Cash tapping into memories of Lee's sense of the absurd to entertain the kids? Or into something long buried inside *himself,* something that being around the kids brought to the surface? Whatever it was, as he continued singing, making the kids laugh harder than they had in way too long—Emma did not remember hearing that last verse before—gratitude rose up inside her for far more than his handiness around the farm.

"Show me, Cash!" Hunter said, about to burst from excitement. "Show me!"

"Now, honey," Emma said, "don't be discouraged if you don't get it right away. Learning to play an instrument takes a lot of practice."

"Your mama's right," Cash said. "I was *terrible* when I started. And for a long time after that. Then again, I didn't have me for a teacher." Emma groaned and Cash grinned at her, and she once more bemoaned the unfairness of life. "Anyway…here's how you make that first G chord," he said, then helped Hunter curl his stubby fingers around the fret. "Now strum the strings with your other hand, like this… Okay, your top finger slipped a little, that's all. There. Now try again."

After two more less-than-stellar tries, Hunter frowned at Cash. "Why can't I make it…sound like when you…play it?"

Cash chuckled. "Because I've been doing this for more than twenty years and you've done it for five minutes. You gotta be patient with yourself, buddy. It'll happen, I promise."

But Hunter scowled at Emma and Zoey. "You two are making me ner-vous. Go away. Please?"

"Yeah, Mama," Cash said, clearly amused, "you're cramping the kid's style."

Clearly *not* amused, Zoey scrambled to her feet and stomped off. "I didn't want to listen to your stupid old lesson, anyway!"

"Zoey!" Emma called, struggling to her feet as Annie scooted out of the kitchen and down the hall, waving her hand in Emma's direction.

"Got it covered, y'all just go on about your business."

"The joys of family life," Emma said without thinking, then flushed. "I'll, uh, be out in the barn if anybody needs me."

Not that anybody would.

The rain had finally stopped, like somebody'd turned off the spigot, encouraging a couple of the nannies to venture forth from their nice, warm happy place to beg for cookies. "Sorry, girls, fresh out," Emma said, earning herself a pair of disgruntled expressions. Of course, that might have something to do with the size of their bellies. Poor gals. But—after a quick inspection—it appeared their misery was about at an end.

If only hers was. In soooo many ways.

Emma went into the barn to check on the others, where lights and heaters gently hummed. Suddenly drained, she lay down in a patch of sunlight from the single, high window, on an eviscerated bale of sweet-scented hay, not even caring when the Smelliest Dog in the Universe collapsed beside her.

And here's where the going-with-the-flow thing and the practical thing don't mesh, she thought, tangling her fingers in the dog's thick fur.

Because she could no longer pretend her feelings weren't growing for Cash. Like weeds. After all, even weeds can be attractive. But every gardener knows you can't let weeds take over, no matter how pretty they might be.

And letting those feelings get out of control, feelings she didn't choose, that she'd been startled to realize she was even ready to entertain so soon after Lee's death…that would be just plain dumb. Even if Cash's return eventually coughed up whatever it was he was looking for, who knew how long it would take before he came to terms with it? If he ever would. Besides which, whether he resumed his career or not, he obviously had no interest in returning to the boonies on a permanent basis.

Crazy, she might be, forming an ill-advised attachment to a man who in all likelihood wasn't even in the same book, let alone on the same page. Not so far gone, however, that she couldn't see that Cash Cochran was about as solid as sand. He barely knew who he was, let alone what he wanted. If—*if*—she were to let another man take root in her heart, it had to be someone ready and willing to commit a hundred percent to her, her kids, this life.

Of his own free will.

Okay, then. *That* settled, Emma nestled more deeply into the hay, pulled Lee's coat closed over her belly and flung one arm around her dog. A few minutes rest, was all she wanted, the goats' soft bleating paving her path to sleepyland…

"Shh, boy," Cash whispered to the dog, who'd jumped to his feet, tail swishing, when Cash walked into the barn. "Don't wake her."

Oh, man. This was bad. Real bad.

Having the hots for a woman, he knew all about. And God knew Emma had provoked the more-than-occasional bite of desire—even in sloppy farm clothes, even a hundred months pregnant, there was no missing the proud-to-be-a-woman sass to her every move. Nothing sexier than a woman who liked her body. And undoubtedly knew what to do with it. But the tender stirrings inside him at the sight of Emma asleep in the sunlight with straw in her hair…

Holy hell. This was worse than those naked-on-stage dreams he had when he was starting out. Especially since those weren't real.

Dodging Bumble's flicking tongue, he crouched beside her. Carefully brushed a snarl of hair off her cheek.

"Emma—?"

She shrieked and sat bolt upright. "What is it? Is everything okay—?"

"Everything's fine. But Zoey came out here, saw you were asleep, and came back to get me. She also said one of the goats was acting funny, so I checked."

She blinked, her reddened cheek creased from the straw. "Somebody's in labor?"

"Yep."

Flailing, she tried to stand, except still half-asleep she couldn't get her bearings. Cash hauled her to her feet, her baby-filled belly crashing into him before she charged unsteadily across the barn, checking each open stall.

"Which one…? Never mind. You mind dragging over that bale so I can sit? Ohmigosh, go get the kids! Mine, I mean."

"You sure?"

"I doubt Myrtle much cares who's watching—"

"Mama!" Zoey said from the barn door. "Is it time?"

"It is, baby," she said, waving Zoey and Hunter over. Zoey squatted beside her mother, her eyes wide, but Hunter hung back beside Cash, slipping his hand inside Cash's. Cash gawked at the kid's head for a second, then squeezed his hand. Hunter looked up, his smile turning his eyes into slits behind his glasses. Then he frowned, focusing again on the kidding goat.

"Does it…hurt her?"

"I'm sure she'd much rather be eating cookies," Emma said, "but it'll be over pretty fast." With a reassuring smile, she stretched to clutch his other hand. "So no worries, okay?"

"Do we need to help?" Zoey asked.

Emma drew her daughter close to lay her cheek on her little girl's head, and the yearning rushed up inside Cash, nearly choking him. "So far everything seems to be going good. In fact…look, guys!"

The first kid slid out onto the straw, shrouded in the birth sac. But before the nanny could lick her baby, she started pushing again.

"What's go-ing on? Is she o-kay, Cash?"

"It's a two-fer," Cash said, chuckling, grabbing a towel from a nearby stack to dry off the newborn. Only Hunter took it from him, vigorously rubbing the kid until it was all fluffy.

"Ma-ma told us we can't let the ba-bies get cold, or they might die."

"Ohmigosh!" Zoey said, giggling, as the kid staggered to its feet with a vague *Whoa, what just happened?* look on its face. "It's *so* cute—!"

"Annnd here's his brother or sister!" Emma said, now on her knees in the straw as the twin slipped out. Only this time Mama was on the case, licking and nudging her baby until he, too, stood on wobbly legs to get a drink. Shortly after, his sister minced over to get her share, and Emma laughed, clearly relieved.

"We have to name them," Hunter said. "How about…Hansel and Gret-el?"

"Done," Emma said, then looked up, and Cash had to armor himself against her twinkling eyes. Her big heart. "One less thing for me to do," she said with a shrug, then wrapped her arms around her son as they watched the babies nurse.

"You're gon-na feed the baby like that, huh?" Hunter said, and Emma sputtered a laugh.

"Not standing up in the barn munching hay, no. But close enough. Okay, nothing else happening here for a while, so you two may as well go do the rest of your chores. I'm gonna stay here with mama and her babies for a while to make sure they're okay. You can visit again later."

As soon as Hunter and Zoey left, though, Emma levered herself back onto the bale to sag against the stall's wall. "One down, five to go. What're the odds the rest of 'em will kid during the day?"

"Slim to none?"

Emma made a sound that might've been a laugh. "Not that it makes much difference, since I'm already up half the night, anyway. Sweet Tater here is into middle-of-the-night aerobics."

"You look beat."

"Comes with the territory," she said, yawning into the back of her hand.

Cash hesitated, then said, "Why don't I bring over a sleeping bag, camp out in the barn until it's over? Save you going back and forth half the night, checking."

"This isn't your problem, Cash—"

"It's not anybody's *problem,*" he said sharply, eyes on the goats and not her. "And tell me Lee wouldn't do the same thing."

"You're not Lee!" When his gaze swung to hers, she sighed out, "I didn't mean that the way it sounded—"

"I know exactly what you mean."

"No, you don't! I'm not comparing you with Lee, Cash. I'd never do that. I just meant you're not in the same position he would've been. As my husband, as co-owner of the farm. None of this is your responsibility. And—"

When she didn't finish her thought, Cash twisted to see her pressing her fingers into the sides of her nose with her eyes shut, shaking her head. "Never mind," she said, as her hands dropped. "It's not that I'm not grateful for the offer, but not being able to take care of my own obligations makes me feel like a wimp. And that's making me *very* cranky."

"Dammit, Emma—why is it so hard for you to let somebody take care of *you?*"

"Probably the same reason it is for you?"

That one landed right between the eyes. Instead of making him mad, though, Cash almost laughed. "Point to you. But you know…for somebody who says she takes things as they come, you sure seem to be mighty picky about which of those things meet your personal criteria. Not that I'm any expert or anything, but I don't think it works that way. Why is it okay if I do other stuff around the farm, but not if I sleep in the barn and keep an eye on the goats?"

Emma stared at him for a moment, then let her head drop back against the stall partition, her mouth pulled into a rueful grin. "I'm being a pain in the butt, huh?"

"That pretty much covers it."

She pushed out a heavy sigh. "Took me five years to talk Lee into the goats. Even so, it was *my* project. Then after he died…I guess I got stubborn, breeding them when I knew how bad the timing would be." A tear slipped out. She swatted it away. "And now I'm exhausted and hormonal and uncomfortable as hell, but I made this particular bed and, dammit, it's mine to lie in and nobody else's!"

Sniffling, she dug a tissue out of her pocket and loudly blew her nose. "Oh, crud, I'm a mess," she said, laughing a little when Bumble laid his head on her lap, nearly knocking her over in the process, and a sudden wave of…of *caring* nearly knocked Cash sideways.

Between being so wrapped up in himself and a talent for picking whiny, helpless women who'd go apoplectic over a broken fingernail, sympathy had never been one of his strong suits. About the only effect women's tears had on him was to annoy him no end. But if it was one thing Emma wasn't, it was whiny. Or helpless. And seeing her this frustrated melted something inside him.

Knowing he was venturing into dangerous territory and completely incapable of stopping, Cash crouched in front of her again, shoving the dog's face out of his. "What you are, is human. And turning yourself inside out to hold it together for everybody else isn't good, for you or the baby. Or anybody else, if you…"

If you end up losing it entirely. Like my mother did.

"So no arguments," he said, letting the sentence dangle. "At least this way you might get *some* sleep. Not to mention I wouldn't have to rat on you to Patrice."

"You wouldn't."

"Oh, believe me, I would." He nodded toward her belly. "He turned yet?"

"No," she said on a sigh, palming the sides of the bulge. Underneath her gigantic sweatshirt, Cash could see movement. Hard to imagine a living human being in there. How tiny it had to be. It occurred to him he'd never actually seen a real live newborn—

"If he's this ornery now," Emma said, her slight smile as she stroked her tummy melting Cash even more, "I can only imagine what he's gonna be like once he's out." Then she chuckled. "I can't wait."

"The term 'glutton for punishment' comes to mind."

"Tell me about it," she said, lifting her eyes, all soft in the hazy light in the stall, and Cash wanted to kiss her so badly, he actually ached.

Instead, he leaned one hand on the bale to balance himself, steering his gaze away from her mouth. From temptation. "Okay, little guy…your mama's kept you warm and safe all for all these months, so there's no reason you can't return the favor. You be good to her, because…" He looked up, caught her startled expression. "Because I know she's gonna be good to you."

Emma flushed a deep scarlet, then looked down. "He got real quiet while you were talking, like he was listening…" She sharply inhaled, her eyes closing. "Early contraction," she got out, her nostrils flaring before she pursed her lips, her breath exiting in a slow, steady stream.

"Looks painful."

She shook her head. "It's all up here," she said, rubbing her palm over the top part of her belly. "So it's just a tightening sensation. No pain. Oh, I forgot! How'd the lesson go?"

Cash stood, her words rekindling the bone-deep satisfaction working with Hunter had given him. "Took a half hour, but Hunter can now play a decent G chord. Tomorrow we'll tackle the C. He already knows the words to the song, though. Although every time he sings it he cracks himself up."

"Sounds about right." Grunting, she flapped about for a second or two, then sighed in disgust.

"Need some help?"

"Gravity sucks," she said, thrusting out her hand. Once on her feet, she dusted off her bottom, then briefly squeezed Cash's arm. "I can't thank you enough for doing this for him. It means a lot, having a man to hang out with. Since Lee died, it's just been us females. Hunter doesn't say anything, but I know he feels a little lost."

Cash frowned. "He got any friends?"

"A couple, from school. But everybody's so scattered and busy, it's hard for the kids to get together. There's a summer camp…" She cleared her throat. "It's for special-needs kids, it wouldn't cost us anything. I'm thinking of sending him for a week. Maybe two." She looked up, her eyes shiny. "He wants to go."

"But you're not sure he's ready?"

"No," she said, looking away. "That I am."

Cash crossed his arms to keep from touching her hair, catching a few threads of fire between his fingers. And when he said, "Why don't you go on inside for a while?" his voice didn't sound right. "Get some more rest, if you can. If anything happens," he said when her mouth opened, "I'll come get you. Promise."

"Okay, deal." She hesitated, her eyes fixed in his, for a couple of seconds before cupping his arm, then reaching up to kiss his cheek, her lips every bit as soft and smooth and warm as they looked. "I sure hope this is half as good for you as it is for me," she said with a twinkly grin, then turned to go, leaving Cash feeling like he'd been clobbered by a thunderbolt.

From one little cheek kiss? Damn.

Damn! He'd forgotten to tell her about his chat with the Garrett brothers.

Then again, Cash thought as he crossed his arms along the top of the stall, watching the kids explore their new world on rapidly strengthening legs, why give her a chance to say no?

Right?

Chapter Seven

"Are you insane?" Emma said. "No!"

Once she got her voice back, that was.

She supposed three more nannies' kidding in the past two days—two of which she actually got to witness—might account for Cash's neglecting to mention he'd hired Noah and Eli Garrett to finish up the job her husband had started. Nothing like walking out her front door this morning to find the brothers leaning against the side of a big, bad, black truck, sipping coffee and shooting the breeze with her, her…whatever the heck Cash was. Farmhand? Savior? Resident pain in the patoot?

"Least you can do is hear me out," Whatever-the-Heck said, shadowing her down rows of lettuces inside the humid greenhouse, only to nearly stumble when she reeled on him, a butter lettuce in each hand. Because, yes, her avoidance method of choice that morning involved seeking succor in the salad greens.

"Why would I do that, when the answer would still be no?"

He scowled. Naturally. "I thought we got this problem about you accepting help cleared up a couple days ago?"

"About you sleeping in my barn, yes. Spending major bucks to remodel my house? No. And why would you do this when you knew how I'd probably react?"

"Because I did it *before* I knew how you'd probably react. Oh, come on, Emma—" His footsteps crunched on the gravel behind her as she tromped over to the next bed. "Give me one good reason why this isn't a good idea."

Emma gently set the lettuces in a bushel basket, then returned to her chore, her knife blade flashing as she efficiently severed the lettuces an inch above the growing point. "Because," she said, wanting to concentrate on lettuces and not crazy, silver-eyed country singers whose generosity was tied to something much deeper inside them than Emma had the wherewithal to explore. She twisted again, meeting those eyes. Drat. "Because it doesn't feel right."

"I said a *good* answer."

By this point she wasn't sure who she was more annoyed with, him or herself for being annoyed. "Sorry, it's the only one I've got. For heaven's sake, Cash," she said when he snorted. "I can't let you spend that kind of money on us."

"Why the hell not? Not like I've got anything else to spend it on."

Through the greenhouse's open door she could see the brothers—both younger than her, both good-looking, one still in his wild stage, the other recently tipped over into settled— patiently waiting for the go-ahead. But how was she supposed to explain something she didn't fully understand herself?

She set the soft, frilly heads in the basket before finally looking at him. And yep, there it was in his eyes—the boy still desperately seeking approval. But for what? And why from her? "Because…because it's like you're trying to buy your own absolution. Or something."

He took the full basket from her, setting it next to the three she'd already filled. "I told you, the money means nothing to me—"

"My point exactly!"

"Dammit, Emma—it's a *gift!*"

"But it's not a gift from your heart. Only from your wallet."

"Oh, for God's sake—"

"And I'd sincerely appreciate it if you didn't take the Lord's name in vain!"

He actually looked startled. "Sorry—"

She swatted away his apology, thinking this conversation was getting more knotted up by the second. Especially since who knew better than she how big Cash's heart actually was, whether he did or not? Still and all, she sensed something seriously amiss about the whole thing, even if she couldn't quite put her finger on it. "Now, if you'd consider this a loan or something…"

Right. As it was, she'd be paying off the uninsured portion of Lee's medical bills until her old age. Taking on more debt was the last thing she needed.

"Not gonna happen," Cash said, right before *Gotcha!* bloomed in his eyes. "You really want me to tell the Garretts to cancel the order? When business has been slow this past year and Eli has a kid on the way, too?"

Emma's own eyes narrowed. "That's low."

"Yeah. Wanting to give Annie a place of her own so you can reclaim your living room, not to mention goosing the local economy, makes me a real bastard." When her voice failed her again, he exhaled. "Maybe you're right, that my wallet's all I got right now. Maybe it's all I'll ever have. What difference does it make to you?"

Emma shut her eyes, shaking her head. Weakening. "It just feels so…lopsided. Like I couldn't even begin to reciprocate."

"You expect people you do things for to reciprocate?"

"No, of course not—"

His gaze nailed her to the spot.

Oh…heck.

The brothers—two of four, all involved in some way in the family business except for the oldest, an accountant—straightened at her approach, offering matching grins. Eli, the newlywed, was the older and more slender of the two, his hair slightly darker and shaggier than his brother's. Noah, whose advice Lee had sought out for help with estimating the materials for the project, was shorter, more solid, and a known heartbreaker, his smile cocky underneath his ball cap's brim.

"You still got the plans Lee drew up?" Emma said to him.

"Right here," he said, wiggling the tube clutched in his hand. "Although…" When his gaze swung to Cash, Emma turned to see Cash trying to shush him. She sighed.

"What?"

"I figured you may as well expand the master bedroom at the same time. Add on a nursery. And maybe a bigger master bath?"

A startled laugh erupted from her throat. "Have you lost your mind? I can't have all that going on with a newborn! And unless y'all are planning on pulling an Extreme Home Makeover number, I'm not seeing it happening within the next two weeks, either."

"Um, Mrs. Manning?" Deep brown, puppy-dog eyes met hers. Strangely, Noah was still grinning. From what she'd heard, that grin made mamas nervous from here to the Colorado border. "Mr. Cochran's already suggested we split up the job, tackling the original remodel project first, starting the other one whenever you're ready. By the time we're finished," he said with an even bigger grin, "you won't even recognize the place. It'll be like having a whole new house!"

Ah.

"Excuse us for a moment, won't you?" she said to the Garretts before steering a confused Cash back to the front porch. "I can't believe it took me this long for the light to dawn," she said, not sure whether to be mad or feel sorry for him or what.

"What light is that?"

"I can understand you wanting to erase the house's bad memories, Cash, I really can. But don't you think erasing the house itself is a bit drastic?"

Cash was so flabbergasted he barely knew what to think. Let alone say. And, oh, it was tempting to think her advanced pregnancy was wreaking serious havoc with her brain function, but not even he was dumb enough to suggest that.

Especially when it occurred to him that maybe she wasn't all that far off the mark.

He sank onto the top step, whisking his hand along his jaw. He hadn't shaved for a couple of days, and the stubble was bugging the hell out of him. Same way the woman currently towering over him was, like some damn redheaded Madonna.

"In my own defense," he muttered, "it wasn't a conscious decision." Perturbed, he squeezed shut his eyes, then lifted them to her. "It's not like I'm ever gonna live here again. And y'all really do need more room. At the front of my brain," he said, tapping his forehead, "this was only about finding some way to do right by Lee, by you, before I returned to my hedonistic ways. That's all. But if I'm being totally honest… the idea of changing the place into something totally different? Doesn't bother me one bit."

She awkwardly lowered herself to sit beside him. "Cash—"

"Yeah, I know…I'm a couple bricks shy of a load." When she looked at him, he shrugged. "Just saving you the trouble."

"That's not what I was gonna say. Even if I might've thought it," she said with a smirk. Then she sighed. "I think it's pretty clear we've both got issues about this remodeling thing. For me, it comes down to…to feeling like I'm being railroaded into something I'm not ready to deal with. For many reasons. Letting go of it as Lee's project being at the top of the list. The timing being seriously bad, for another."

Cash leaned forward. Scratched his head. Sighed. "You're right. I should've thought of that. All of it."

She touched his arm. Briefly. "The thing is, I'd love more room. Someday. Just not now. Not…yet. And you—"

"I'm not doing this for myself, Emma," Cash said softly. "I swear. I really was only thinking of you."

"I believe you. No, I do. I was overreacting."

"To what?"

Swiping back her hair, she angled her head. "You're an incredibly generous man, Cash. All that eagerness to please… it can be kind of overwhelming."

His face heating, Cash got to his feet. "I'll tell the Garretts to hold off, then, until you're ready. Don't worry, they can keep the deposit. Since they were going to fit in the job as a favor, anyway, later might be better for them, too."

Her eyes softened. "Thank you."

"No problem," he said, walking away, thinking if all good deeds were this hard to pull off, no wonder so few people bothered.

Thirty-eight weeks and still not engaged.

The baby, that was. Little booger was still upside down, too, far as Emma knew, but as long as he was still floating, there was hope.

"Annie?" Emma called down the hall. "You about ready?"

"One last tinkle and I'm good. You go on ahead, I'll meet you at the car. My stuff's by the door."

Feeling like a wind-up toy run up against a wall—going and going and getting nowhere fast—Emma inched toward the front door, grabbing her purse and keys off the hall table before lugging Annie's paint box and canvas out to the car. As she shoved everything inside, though, she took a moment to savor the bright blue sky, fields greening up, her emperor tulips swaying in the warm breeze. All baby goats were birthed and doing well, including three sets of twins. Sales had been brisk, her CSA clients seemed pleased, and overall things were improving.

Well, except for that pesky falling-for-the-help thing, she thought as she looked toward the north field, where Cash and a couple of locals he'd Pied Pipered in from Ortega's a few days ago were mulching the berry canes to keep their little tootsies from freezing during the still-cold nights.

He looked up and waved, his smile tenuous. Emma waved back, her dumbbutt heart pitty-pattying inside her chest. She'd meant what she'd said, about his overwhelming generosity. Whatever his motives, the effect was the same on her heart, worn down from grief and worry and loneliness. Not desperation, though. Praise be, she was still clearheaded enough not to act like a fool, even if she felt like one.

To recognize, for instance, that his new "thing" of performing for them in the lengthening evenings, before he returned to his place, was only a signal that the real world, *his* real world—illusive or not—had begun tugging him back.

That the more he healed, the less reason he had to stay.

Which was why part of her sorely wished he'd just go away, already, and let her get on with things…before that paper-thin barrier between silly and stupid dissolved completely.

Annie and several cats burst through the front door, derailing Emma's train of thought to nowhere; some twenty minutes later Emma dropped her off at her art teacher's house in town, a funky little adobe with a studio out back.

"Now remember," Annie said as she wrestled all her paraphernalia out of the car, "pick me up right at two! Can't miss Oprah!"

"Yes, ma'am," Emma said with a little salute. She watched the old woman until she'd disappeared inside the house, then backed out of the driveway, realizing she had four whole hours with nowhere to be, nobody to feed and nothing to pick. Sweet.

Twenty minutes later, wrapped up in Lee's old robe, she balanced—precariously—on the edge of the hall bath's tub, banging loose a clod of ancient, powdered bubble bath, then crumbling it underneath the stream of hot water as it pounded into the old tub. Her eyes closed, she deeply inhaled the gardenia-scented steam. When was the last time she'd had a real bath, instead of her usual in-and-out shower? She couldn't remember.

Just in case, she set her cell phone on the toilet seat where she could reach it, shoved The Red One's paws off the tub's rim, then dropped the robe. With a blissful sigh, she lowered herself into the bubbles, laughing when suds and water sloshed overboard, sending at least three cats streaking for cover. Not that she could exactly soak—she was far too big and the tub far too small—but it was better than a stick in the eye. And bit by bit, Emma felt her muscles go limp, the warm, soap-slippery water gliding over her undulating belly, like the baby couldn't wait to break out into a larger pool. She laughed softly, skimming a hand over the slick bulge before drifting into a light doze.

A few minutes later she awoke with a start, the water chilly and the bubbles mostly gone, regretfully musing how the good things in life never seemed to last long enough. Like ice cream cones. Sex. Warm baths.

Husbands.

"And you can get off *that* road right now," Emma muttered, hooking one hand over the edge of the tub to hoist herself out.

Except the one-hand-hoist thing didn't work so well when your belly'd turned into a forty-pound beach ball. Grunting a little, she tried shifting onto her hip, only to discover the tub seemed a lot narrower than she remembered. And slipperier.

"Okay, don't panic," she said, panicking, as she realized that no matter which way she tried to turn, any number of laws of physics had conspired against her.

In other words, she was stuck. Naked, hugely pregnant and stuck in a bathtub she'd no business getting into to begin with.

Yeah, let's hear it for hindsight, she thought, gazing at the half dozen or so cats who'd wandered in to watch the festivities, each wearing a little kitty smirk on its fuzzy, smug face. The Black Spotted One came over to stand with his paws on the edge of the tub, did a quick take of the situation, then looked at her as if to say, *Sucks for you, huh?*

Emma flicked water at the thing, then tried once more to pry herself out. Nothing doing. If anything, she was probably swelling up like a sponge from sitting so long in the water. Realizing there was only one person near enough to help her, she looked at the phone and sighed.

One day I'll laugh about this, she thought, and dialed.

"Emma?" Cash called out when he banged open the front door, fighting Bumble for first right of entry. "Where are you?"

"Bathroom," he heard from down the hall. His heart pounding—she'd said she was stuck and couldn't get up—he raced through the house, Bumble slipping and sliding beside him, only to find himself facing an empty, puddled room, dotted with the occasional cat.

"Where—?"

"In here," she said from behind the quivering, aquarium-themed shower curtain. Bumble trotted over to check, then woofed, like *Yep, that's her all right.*

"You're in the tub?"

"Uh, yeah."

Cash paused. "As in—?"

"Yep."

"Oh." His chest started to tickle with the effort not to laugh. "Wow. This is embarrassing."

"You're telling me. And don't think I didn't consider staying right here until the baby comes. Are you laughing?"

"Wouldn't d-dream of it."

"Don't think I've ever heard you laugh before."

"It might've been a while," Cash said as the chuckle erupted.

He heard a sigh. "Okay, hand me the robe, I'll put it on as best I can and then you can help me out of here."

Cash scooped up the robe from the floor, threading it behind the edge of the vinyl curtain, where an unseen force snatched it away.

"And here I thought I was gonna get to see you naked."

"You did *not* just say that."

Whoa. Sun must've been a lot hotter than he realized. "Apparently, I did."

"You'd probably be scarred for life." The curtain shimmied. "Trust me, this is a *lot* of naked."

"And this would be a problem, why?"

The metal rings screeched as Emma shoved the curtain back from the bottom. Looking highly chagrined, she sat in the tub with the robe haphazardly wrapped around her, covering the best bits. The dog seemed determined to get in the tub with her. "Because we don't have that kind of relationship?"

"We do now." Cash frowned at her. "How should we do this?"

"Not sure. Although getting rid of the dog—Bumble, for crying out loud!—might be a good first step."

After a good thirty seconds of wrestling with and cussing at a hundred-pound dog determined to guard his mistress, Cash had banished Bumble and approached the tub again, ignoring the periodic WHOMP! as the whining dog tried to break down the door. Then, before he could reconsider or Emma could protest, he stepped in behind her, grabbed her under the arms and hauled her to her feet, after which he stepped back out, handed her a towel and left. Although he—and Bumble—stayed close by. Just in case.

"You still there?" she called from inside.

"Hell, yeah. How're you doing?"

"Fine. Now." A pause. "Thanks."

"No problem." Cash grinned. "You still embarrassed?"

"Did you see anything you weren't supposed to?"

"Unfortunately, no."

Then she laughed. That full, rich laugh that shoved him a little bit further down that road. "And you lie like a rug."

He leaned closer to the door and said in a low voice, "And you have absolutely nothing to be embarrassed about—"

"Uh-oh."

Cash froze. "Em? Everything okay?"

"Other than the fact that the floor's even wetter than it was? Sure thing."

"I don't understa—"

He jumped back when the door wrenched open and Emma plowed past him. "Baby's coming," she said, and Cash felt all the blood drain from his face.

Chapter Eight

"Now?" he said as Emma disappeared into her bedroom.

"Call Patrice. Her number's right by the kitchen phone. Oh, shoot—I need somebody to pick up Annie from her art class—"

"What about the kids?"

More or less clothed, she zoomed from the room, headed for the kitchen, moving faster than he'd ever seen her. Cash, however, felt nailed to the floor.

"They'll be okay, the bus'll bring 'em home as usual."

"Emma?"

"Yeah?"

"The baby...did he ever turn around?"

She appeared at the kitchen doorway, eyes wide, hair wild. "I don't know, I'll have to wait until Patrice gets here be-before I know f-for sure. Cripes, there I g-go," she said, laughing a little. "Soon as my water breaks, I start shaking like a leaf. Happens every time."

Then she burst into tears. Crap. He should do something. Make her sit? Boil water? Hold her? But when he tried, she waved him off. "No, it's okay, I'm fine. You go call Patrice. Then would you mind going into town to get Annie?"

"No way am I leaving you alone."

There. A decision. He could do this.

She opened her mouth, then seemed to think better of it. "Okay, we'll wait for Patty, then you go get Annie. Ohmigosh—" Her floaty, tentlike shirt rippling around her hips, she took off for the living room like a flustered moth, stumbling over Bumble and scattering cats as she snatched magazines and clothes off the furniture. "The house is a holy mess. I'd planned on cleaning tomorrow—"

Cash grabbed her shoulders, steering her toward the sofa. "I'll straighten up after I call Patrice, you sit—"

"No," she said, squirming out of his grasp, "I have to do something, I have to... Whoa, *baby*," she said, suddenly grabbing the back of the chair and bending over, blowing out her breath in short pants. A brief *Oh, hell* moment passed, leaving a surprisingly steady calm in its wake. That they'd all get through this. That Lee would be relieved to know Emma wasn't alone.

Almost like he knew what he was doing, Cash leaned beside her, firmly stroking her back, breathing with her. When it was over, she blew out a long breath, then a shaky laugh. "Right now I wish I was a goat."

"Right now I wish you were, too," Cash said, and she laughed again, then looked up at him, so much honesty and trust in her eyes he thought his chest would cave in.

"It's gonna be okay," he said, and she smiled.

"No doubt. But go. Call," she said, continuing to clean. "If that contraction was anything to go by, this won't take long."

Cash didn't exactly find that assessment reassuring.

* * *

Even before Patrice met her eyes after the exam, Emma knew.

"He's still facing the wrong way?"

"He's down too far to tell," the midwife said, sighing. "I hate to send you to the hospital for an ultrasound to be sure, but I don't want to take a chance. When was the last contraction?"

Sitting up, Emma checked the clock. "Nearly ten minutes ago. But it was so strong, I thought…"

"Sometimes the first one after the water breaks is strong," Patrice said gently, "but then things get all disorganized for a little while."

"Right. I knew that."

Patrice squeezed her knee. "Cash went to get Annie?"

Emma nodded, suddenly missing Lee so much she hurt. Wanting Cash so much she hurt more. Tears burned at the backs of her eyes; Patrice slung an arm around her shoulders and gave her a hug. "Listen to me—there's a whole mess of people to get your back. And that Cash is right at the front of the pack."

She half laughed. "I hardly think—"

"And maybe you should stop thinking so much and open your eyes, see what's right in front of your face. I saw how he looked at you, right before he went out that door."

"You mean the scared-out-of-his-wits look?"

"If he didn't care he wouldn't be scared."

"And somebody's been watching way too many chick flicks. Cash is only here out of some sense of obligation to Lee, Patty."

"Yeah, well," the midwife said, getting to her feet, "maybe that's how it started out, but now I'm betting he sees some-

thing he wants—and needs—real bad. And if you ask me—"
she went into the bathroom to wash her hands "—the feeling's mutual—"

At least that was what Emma thought she said, since another contraction diverted her attention for a minute. Shaking
her hands dry, Patrice returned from the bathroom to palm
Emma's stomach.

"How was it?"

"Fair," she said, standing, "Forty-five seconds, maybe a
little longer since I missed the start."

The front door slammed. Not five seconds later Annie
appeared at the doorway, Cash behind her. Her eyes were lit
up like a pair of Christmas bulbs, only to dim for a moment
when Emma told her the baby probably wouldn't be born
there. Then she brightened again.

"So I'll come to the hospital with you!"

"Then who's gonna stay with the kids?"

"Oh, yeah. But that's okay—I can spoil 'em rotten without
you givin' me the evil eye."

Again, tears flooded Emma's eyes as she pulled Annie into
a hug. "I love you so much, old woman, you know that?"

Annie hugged her back, then released her, her own eyes
as wet as Emma's. "I love you, too, sweet girl. If it wasn't for
you, I'd probably be in some crappy home eatin' dried-up pork
chops and gray green beans every night."

From the doorway, Cash cleared his throat. "Patrice said
it'd probably be better if I took you, since my car actually has
shocks."

It was true. Between Patrice and Emma they probably
wouldn't get a buck-fifty for all three of their vehicles put
together—

"What's go-ing on?" Hunter asked as he and Zoey crashed
through the door. "Why's Pat-ty's truck out-side?"

"The baby's coming," Emma said softly. "Cash is going to take me to the hospital—"

"The *hos-pital?* No!" Hunter rushed her, grabbing her around the middle. "You said you were gon-na have the baby right here, where we could see him come out!" He lifted distressed eyes to hers. "You promised, no hospital! *No hos-pital!*"

"Sweetie, I didn't actually promise…" She hissed in a breath between her teeth as another contraction hit, stronger this time. Riding the wave, she breathed through it, holding on to Hunter for support but still in control enough to offer him a half smile. Because while she'd prepared them for witnessing their brother's birth, she hadn't prepared them for the possibility that she wouldn't have the baby at home. Nor had it struck her until this very moment what "going to the hospital" meant to her nearly panicked son.

Because the last time one of his parents went to the hospital, he didn't come back.

Zoey wasn't sure if the white-hot-scared feeling in the pit of her stomach came from her own brain or from the look in her brother's eyes. She thought maybe she should say something to make him feel better, especially since Patrice and Granny were busy rubbing Mama's back while she panted, but what that was, she had no idea.

So when Cash bent in front of them, putting a hand on each of their shoulders? Boy, was she glad. 'Course, he looked a little worried, too, like maybe he wasn't sure what he was supposed to say, either. But soon as he looked in Zoey's eyes she felt a whole lot better.

"What your mama's doing," he said in a low voice, "it's exactly like what happened with the goats—"

"Then why's she gotta go to the *hos-pital?*" Hunter whined, holding Zoey's hand and shaking from head to toe.

"So they can make sure the baby's going to come out the right way," Cash said softly. "Because if he isn't, it's not safe for her to have him here—"

"So if she goes to the hos-pital, they can fix it?" Hunter said, but almost before Cash could say, "Yes," Hunter shook his head, hard, and said, "That's what Ma-ma said when they took Daddy there. That they could fix him. On-ly they didn't. And he *died*."

Zoey was trying to be brave, she really was, but Hunter's saying that made the bad feeling get all burny, like right before you throw up. She didn't, but she started shaking, too. And crying. Like some dumb baby.

"Hey, hey, hey…" Cash said, squatting in front of them now and speaking in a real soft voice. Then he reached behind him for the box of tissues on the end table so they could each get one. "Your daddy was sick. Sicker than anybody knew. He didn't die because he went to the hospital, he died because his heart was too busted up for them *to* fix.

"But that's not what's going on with your mama. Remember when I had to help Sweet Pea get her baby out? Your mama's going where they have more people who can help her and the baby—"

"I wanna go, too!" Zoey said, wiping away the snot. "I wanna be there when the baby's born!"

"Me, too—"

"You can't, sugars," Mama said, coming to sit on the sofa in front of them. Zoey had been so busy crying and stuff she hadn't noticed that Mama had finished getting dressed and braided her hair, like she was fixing to go to the store or something instead of the hospital. She was smiling, too, her eyes all bright, like she was excited. "Not yet, anyway," she said, grabbing both Zoey's and Hunter's hands. "Not until… not until we know how this is all gonna play out. Besides, if you guys come with me, who's gonna feed the goats?"

Zoey'd forgotten about the goats. "Can we give them a cook-ie?" Hunter asked.

"One each," Mama said, trying to sound stern. "No more."

Then a little lightbulb flashed in Zoey's brain. "If you're not back by tomorrow, do we hafta go to school?"

Now Mama laughed right out loud, and Zoey remembered that when Daddy had gone to the hospital, Mama had definitely not been laughing. "No. Tomorrow is definitely a school holiday. So. Are we good?"

Zoey nodded so hard she thought her head might come off. Hunter didn't look so sure, though. Zoey guessed he didn't remember about Mama not laughing before. But before she could say something, Cash hugged Hunter real hard, then looked right at him and said, "Everything's gonna be fine, big guy. I swear." Then he looked over at Mama with a funny look on his face, and another lightbulb went off, that Cash loved them. Mama and Hunter and her and Granny…all of them.

Even if he didn't know it yet.

Cash took Emma's silence on the way to the hospital to mean one of two things: either she was concentrating real hard on having this baby, or she was pissed at him for saying what he had to the kids. Or both. And, yes, pondering that took his mind off the fact that he was driving a woman in labor to the hospital. Crazy.

"Is it okay to talk?" he finally asked.

"And take my mind off what's about to happen?" Emma said with a little laugh. "You bet." She looked over. "What's up?"

"I probably shouldn't've promised the kids everything would be okay. Not that I don't think it will be," he quickly added, "but promises are courting trouble."

"I know," she said on a sigh. "But I don't want them to spend their childhood thinking the boogeyman is lurking in every corner either, that they can't trust happiness. I want them to believe there's more good in life than bad. And yet…"

She tugged her long braid around, toying with the feathery end. "It tears me up that I can't give them back their innocence. That I *can't* promise that the baby and I will be fine."

His stomach cramped. "Are you…scared?"

"For myself? Not particularly. For them, for this baby…" A soft sigh preceded, "It's not like I was some sheltered little thing before Lee's death. Heaven knows I'm no stranger to challenges. But him dying…even until the end, I didn't believe it. I kept thinking he'd somehow pull out of it, because he was Lee. When he didn't…it rocked my world harder than I thought possible."

"That's quite an admission, coming from you."

"Heh. Just because I don't crumble in the face of disaster doesn't mean I'm impervious to it."

"And let me guess—nobody knew how much you were hurting."

"Not really. Don't get me wrong—I cried my heart out at first. And I made sure the kids knew it was okay to be sad. Even so, it was like no matter how much I grieved, it was never enough to relieve the pain."

Cash paused. "You still grieving?"

"No," she said quickly, quietly, not looking at him. "The pain finally went away of its own accord. Mostly. Not that I don't still miss Lee. Especially now," she said, stroking her belly. "But what I didn't expect was that, when the pain went away? It took part of me with it. Like the kids' innocence, I suppose, but…I don't know how to explain it. Other than I'm not the same person I was before. And sometimes that makes me sad. If not…more than a little mad. Okay, here's another one," she said, gripping the armrest between them and slowly breathing through the contraction.

When she breathed out that last, cleansing breath, Cash said, "We've got another ten minutes, probably, before we get there—"

"Not to worry. It's not serious until it feels like somebody's trying to set fire to your crotch."

Cash winced, then said, "It's early yet."

"I know, that's what I was saying—"

"I'm not talking about the baby, I'm talking about…Lee." He glanced at her, then back at the road. "He hasn't even been gone a year. Maybe…maybe that part of you that feels like it's gone missing is just on vacation. So it'll probably come back at some point."

Probably a good ten seconds passed before Emma said, very softly, "That mean you're still waiting, too?" He felt her eyes, gentle on the side of his face. "Even after more than twenty years?"

Cash almost smiled. "How do you manage to turn everything I say back on me?"

"It's a talent," she said, then let out a gasp, followed by some truly vicious panting, and it pained him to see her in pain.

"Almost there," he said, even though they weren't.

"Good," she said, even though something told him it wasn't.

"They're both fine," Cash said to Annie into his cell phone, leaning against the pale green wall outside Emma's hospital door. Relaxed on the outside, practically vibrating on the in-side from the leftover adrenaline. Now he remembered why he generally avoided attachments. Why he was the least likely candidate for "family man" you could name. "Although Em's real bummed she couldn't have him naturally."

"So the baby never turned?"

"Actually, he did. But he was so big he got stuck."

"How big are we talking?"

"A shade over ten pounds. They're both okay, though," he repeated as another wave of adrenaline shuddered through. "Which is the important thing."

"And you?"

"I'm fine."

Now.

"You see the baby?"

"Sure, they brought him in with her, although they're both asleep. Damn, Annie…he looks exactly like Lee," Cash said, choking up. Again. "Blond hair and all." He chuckled, even as his eyes stung. "Fattest cheeks you ever saw. I got a couple of pics on my phone—"

"Go ahead and send 'em so I can show the kids. Cash… Emma's gonna need a lot more help than we'd figured. She's not gonna be able to get right up after a C-section and haul around hay bales or full bushels of crops. Not to mention taking care of the house. I can cook and all, but I'm not sure I'm up to lugging around a ten-pound baby. And he won't stay ten pounds for long! So if you could find it in your heart to stick around, we'd sure appreciate it."

Cash froze. "Annie, I don't know a damn thing about babies—"

"You'd be surprised, how little the baby will care. I know Em wanted her mother to come, but she won't leave Emma's daddy. He has that Alzheimer's, you know."

"Yeah, she told me." He turned, leaning one palm on the wall, staring at his boot top. "How long are we talking?"

"Well, Lee was a section baby and they told his mama she couldn't strain herself for at least six weeks. I doubt things have changed much since then. Oh, Lord, Hunter's about to rupture something with wanting to talk to you himself—"

"Is my ma-ma okay, Mr. Cash?"

"She sure is—" Surely Emma wouldn't expect Cash to hang around that long, would she? "—although since they had to operate to get the baby out safely, she has to stay in the hospital a few days. And then…" He shut his eyes. "Then she's gonna have to take it easy for a while after she gets back home."

"Who's gon-na take care of the ba-by, then?"

"I guess we'll all have to help her," Cash said as the calm mercifully claimed him again, shepherding him gently, but firmly, past the fear. "Hold on, Hunter, I'm sending you a picture of the baby…there. Did you get it?"

He heard Zoey's giggle and Annie's, "Oh, land—he does look exactly like Lee!" before Hunter came back on the line with, "He's real cute, huh?"

"I guess he is," Cash said, interrupted by Zoey's, "When can we come see Mama?" in the background. "Tell your sister I'll bring all of you to see your mama and the baby tomorrow, after they've both had a chance to rest up some. How's that?"

Slipping his phone back into his pocket, Cash wondered, with a bittersweet ache that verged on torturous, how he'd let himself get sucked deeper and deeper into this family that wasn't his.

How to extricate himself before any lasting damage was done.

Because all he was, was a placeholder. A stand-in, like somebody dragged in from the crew to stand on stage while the lighting dudes fiddled with levels and angles when the star wasn't there.

Then he ducked back into Emma's room, and she stirred in her sleep, smiling, and he knew he could no more leave this woman in a lurch than he could have flown.

"You stuck around?" she said, her words slightly slurred.

"How'd you know it was me?"

"Cowboy boots. Nurses don't wear 'em."

Shoving his hands in his back pockets, Cash stood at the foot of her bed. Seeing Emma this vulnerable, in a hospital bed with the IV tube still attached...it was strange. And discomfiting. "Dumb question, but how are you feeling?"

She laughed softly, her eyes opening, although they seemed a trifle unfocused. "There's happy juice in that there tube. Any time I want a hit all I have to do is press this cute little button. So right now I'm feeling pretty darned good."

"Been pressing the button a lot, have you?"

Her eyes drifted closed again, a half smile curving her lips. "Mmm-hmm." Then she waved vaguely toward the baby in the clear-sided bassinet nearby, all wrapped up in a striped blanket like a little sausage. "Bring Skye over so I can see 'im."

Cash's heart jackknifed. "You sure?"

"Mmm-hmm." More awake now, she carefully shifted to lie on her side. "You can't break him. I promise. One hand under his head, the other under his butt. He probably won't even wake up."

He didn't, although his tiny forehead puckered when Cash clumsily lifted him out of the bassinet. Instinctively Cash tucked the baby against his suddenly tight chest, a million thoughts and emotions bombarding him. He hadn't signed on for this, when he'd decided to come looking for Lee....

"You look good like that," Emma said.

"Except for the part about not being able to move?"

She smiled. "Put one foot in front of the other...yeah, like that...hey, there, Bruiser," she crooned as Cash gently lowered

Skye into her arms. Her mouth trembling, she kissed his tiny fingers, then unwrapped the blanket to chuckle at his shapeless feet. "He's absolutely gorgeous, isn't he?" she said.

Right before she dissolved into tears.

Like he was being shoved from behind, Cash stumbled closer, only to jerk to a stop a foot away, again having no idea what to do. What to say. But, man, it was ripping him apart, seeing her so unhappy.

"Sorry," Emma mumbled, trying to reach for the tissues on the nightstand. Cash's paralysis gave way enough for him to hand her the box. "You'd think eight months would be enough to prepare me f-for..." Tears running down her cheeks, she touched the baby's face, shaking her head.

"It's not right," Cash finally pushed out past the knot at the base of his throat. "Lee's the one who should be here. Not me."

Emma sagged farther into the pillows, her gaze fixed on the baby. "I'd forgotten, how all I want to do is stare at them after they're born." She dabbed her eyes with the tissue, blew her nose. Took a deep, shaky breath before cuddling her newborn closer. "Cash...there'd be something wrong with me if I wasn't missing my baby's daddy right now. But..."

She lifted her eyes, her mouth pulled into a sad smile. "But thinking about the 'shoulds' is pointless. I loved Lee with all my heart, but he's gone. And for whatever reason, it *is* you here with me right now. It was you keeping watch over me and this baby, over all of us, these past few weeks. And I'm more grateful for that than I can say. I think Lee would be, too. You've been a true friend. As much to us as you were to Lee."

Smiling more easily now, she lowered her eyes again to the baby. "No wonder he talked my ear off about you. You're no ordinary man, Cash, and that's the truth."

Now a paralysis of a different kind slowed his blood. "That's the joy juice talking."

She laughed, sweeping her loose hair behind her shoulder. Except it slipped right back, half covering the baby. "Maybe the joy juice is giving me the courage to say all that," she said, curling her fingers around his hand, "but it's true. Every word. Isn't that right, Skye? We don't know how we would've made it through without you."

"Boy. All kinds of admissions coming out of you today."

At last she looked up. "Enjoy it while you can."

"Then..." His heart hammered. "I trust you won't give me grief about sticking around for a while. Annie says it'll be six weeks, at least, before you'll be back to normal."

Emma frowned. "Annie asked you to stay?"

"More or less."

"And you said yes?"

"I didn't say no."

The pillows crinkled slightly when she leaned into them again. "She shouldn't have done that. Don't you have a life of your own to get back to?"

"You trying to run me off?"

"Not at all. But I don't want you to feel obligated simply because Annie asked."

"I'd be doing it for you, not for Annie!" Cash said, not entirely sure why he was suddenly so pissed. "I don't..." He sucked in a breath. "I don't break promises—"

"But you didn't—"

"Let me finish, Emma. Please. I've never once cut a tour short, or walked out of a recording session, or even stopped working on a song I believed in just because it got hard." He rammed his hands into his pockets again. "Or been the one to end a relationship, other than the one with my father. The women all left me. I can't help it, leaving things unfinished drives me nuts."

Under Emma's steady gaze, he took that last step to curve his hand around Skye's head, all cozy in a little knit cap. Through a barrage of emotions, he said, "I promised to stay until you were on your feet. To be honest, I'm not sure if I made that promise to you or Lee or myself, or maybe even something higher, but I made it." His eyes touched hers. "That it's taking longer than anybody figured is immaterial. But believe me…when it's time for me to go, we'll both know it."

After a long pause, she nodded. "Fair enough, then. And it's not like I won't be grateful for the help. See?" she said, grinning. "I can be taught. Although you do realize it means staying in the house?"

He almost smiled. "I think it's safe to say the tub incident pretty much put paid to those issues. If I was looking for memories to replace the bad ones, that one definitely did the trick."

Her laugh reached deep inside him, tugging him that much closer. Conflicting him that much more. "I suppose…Hunter can bunk with Zoey for a few weeks, so you can have his room. And no arguments. Trust me, Hunter will find it more than a fair trade."

"Then…it's settled," Cash said, thinking *settled* was the last thing he was feeling at the moment. Moth to the flame, was what came to mind. "I'll tell the others what we've decided. I already said they can come visit tomorrow, if that's okay with you?"

"Of course—"

"But…I could come back tonight, if you want?"

A beat or two passed before she said, "You've done enough for one day. Especially since we're going to be seeing plenty of each other over the next few weeks."

Apprehension seized his lungs, even as he gently clasped her shoulder, bent to kiss her hairline. Questioning, tired eyes met his, probably mirroring his own. "See you tomorrow, then," he said, backing away.

"Sounds good," she said, and he booked it out of there, his heart thumping as he rode down the elevator, people's heads turning as he practically raced through the lobby and out toward the parking lot. Deep down, he knew staying and seeing this through was right. Possibly the most right thing he'd ever done.

But if that was true, why did it feel so very, very wrong?

Chapter Nine

Four days after giving birth, Emma gingerly scaled her front porch steps past a very excited Bumble to a welcome-home party that would make any mother proud. Tired to think about, but proud. Hunter and Zoey had even gone all out with a "Welcome Home, Baby Skye!" banner painted in a rainbow of colors on what Emma sincerely hoped was an *old* sheet. Jewel and Patrice were there, as well as a smattering of church ladies and Annie's fellow art students, none of whom was under seventy, and they were all wearing party hats left over from—Emma squinted, then laughed, even though it hurt—New Year's Eve seven years ago.

There was more food than they'd be able to eat in a month, of course, and presents for the baby, and in the middle of it all Cash, toting Skye in his car seat, seemingly unfazed by his lone-rooster-in-the-henhouse status.

What am I going to do with you? Emma thought as he steered her toward the living-room sofa, solicitousness personified. And how on earth was she gonna survive another six weeks of his presence? Although there'd been no more of that kissing stuff—impossible in any case since they hadn't been alone since—something sure as shootin' had shifted between them the instant his lips made contact. Something she highly doubted was going to make things *easier*.

"We have a surprise!" Annie said, and Emma groaned. Once her happy juice supply had been cut off, reality had hit. As in, she was sore and weak and basically grumpy as heck, especially now that her milk was in and Bruiser took her for a 7-Eleven.

"I'm truly touched, everybody, but I'm not exactly up for a party—"

"I think you'll be up for this," Annie said, then said, "She's here, you can come out now," and the next thing Emma knew her mother was walking toward her with her arms out, and all thoughts of Cash went flying right the window. Most of 'em, anyway. Emma gasped, squeaked and started to cry. For at least the thousandth time since the birth. If there was a correlation between tears shed and pounds lost, she'd look like a supermodel by Tuesday.

"How on earth—?" she soggily mumbled into her mother's striped jersey blouse, inhaling the familiar blend of shea butter and Aqua Net. Although less padded than Emma, Gayle Stoddard's nearly six-foot-tall frame and more-is-more makeup philosophy had been known to give off the occasional drag-queen vibe. Except Mama did not subject her size-12 feet to the torture of four-inch heels.

Now her mother gave her an equally waterlogged smile. "Never you mind," she said, patting Emma's hand. "The important thing is, I'm here. Now let me see this little guy— ohmigosh!" she said, unstrapping Skye from his seat and settling on the sofa with the sleeping baby on his back on her sturdy lap. Then she grinned at her other grandchildren. "He's bigger than the two of you were put together!"

Then she went on and on, prattling to the baby, about the baby, like there was nothing remotely extraordinary about her visit. Soon as the shindig broke up an hour later, though, and Cash and the kids went off to do chores, Emma decided Mama had some splainin' to do.

"Not that I'm not thrilled," she said from the kitchen table while her mother wrapped and cleaned and clucked over some of the more adventurous offerings. Beside Emma, Bumble kept looking back and forth between her and the sleeping Skye in his seat on the floor. *Have no clue what this thing is, but no worries, I keep it safe, promise.* "But barely a week ago you said you couldn't make it. And now you're here."

"Just for the weekend," Gayle said, her back to Emma as she half-heartedly shooed cats. "I assume it's okay if I share your bed? Since Hunter said he's staying in Zoey's room while Cash is here?"

"Yeah…about that. Cash wouldn't have anything to do with this, would he?"

Mama turned, munching on a cheesy…something. "I swear, I had no idea you didn't know. But yes. Well, he and Annie, both. It was Cash who called me, though, right after the baby came, asked if there was any way I could get out there, even if only for a couple of days."

"Because he wasn't exactly down with playing new baby nurse?"

Chewing, her mother shook her head, then smiled. "I'm guessing there would've been more panic in his voice if that'd been the case."

"But…what about Daddy?"

"Actually, honey…" Mama lowered herself into the chair opposite, her hands in her lap and guilt clouding her eyes.

"Bill's... I moved him into one of those homes, for people with Alzheimer's? Someplace where they can keep a much better eye on him than I can."

Emma stared at her mother for a moment, waiting out the dizziness. "When did this happen? And why on earth didn't you tell me?"

"Six months ago. And I didn't tell you because...because I had to sell the house. To cover the initial fees."

"Mama!"

"Don't you 'Mama' me, you had enough on your plate without worrying about me, too. And don't give me that look, it's not like I'm out on the street or anything. I've got an adorable little apartment close to your father—in fact," she said, digging her cell phone out of her pocket and scooting across the table to Emma. "I took pictures before I left." While Emma scrolled through the photos, dazed, Mama said, "Anyway, the plain truth is, since I don't drive long distances much anymore, and spur-of-the-moment plane tickets are through the roof—"

"Cash bought you one."

"Yes. He did. Which I didn't know until I opened my e-mail two days ago and there it was." Curiosity flickered in her eyes. "Under ordinary circumstances, I'd say the man was sweet on you. But now I'm guessing these aren't ordinary circumstances?"

Returning the phone to her mother, Emma released a weary laugh. Mama sat back in her chair, her arms crossed over her double Ds. "You sweet on him?"

"Don't go getting that gleam in your eye," Emma said, carefully pushing herself up from the table. Bumble scrambled to his feet, then sat again, eyes on the baby. Emma half wondered if the dog would let her have him back. "Cash is a very giving, very troubled man who's here for his own reasons. We've already agreed, when I'm back on my feet, he's outta here. And, no, I'm not about to try changing his mind."

Her arms still crossed, her mother gave her The Eye. "Why do I get the feeling you're not entirely happy about that?"

"Mama, I love you. And I'm more grateful than I can say that you're here. But I'm far too wiped out to get into this with you or anybody else." She yawned. "In fact, I'm going to go crawl into bed with my baby and my dog. Would you mind bringing Skye…?"

But before she could get around the table, her mother was up, pulling Emma into her arms for a gentle hug. And, yep, that got the waterworks flowing all over again.

Pocketing his car keys, Cash walked back into the house after taking Gayle to the airport, and it smelled like coffee and vanilla candles and fabric softener, like *Emma,* and it struck him—not for the first time—that whatever defined the place as belonging to her, and her family, really had thoroughly washed away every trace of his father, of the old memories. Not that Cash couldn't still conjure them up, but they weren't in his face anymore. Couldn't hurt him anymore.

When they'd started to dissolve, he had no idea. Around when he started giving Hunter his guitar lessons, maybe. But by the time he'd moved his things into the boy's brightly colored bedroom, spent his first night in Hunter's double bed with its jungle-animal-motif bedding, he'd finally stopped thinking of this as his home.

Instead, he realized as The Calico One bounced up on her hind legs to meet his hand when he reached over to pet her, he was now a guest in someone else's.

He found Emma in the kitchen—*her* kitchen—the baby in his little bouncy seat on the table in front of her, Bumble comatose as usual at her feet. Dressed in one of her roomy tops, her hair loosely coiled at the back of her head, she was frowning at her open laptop, periodically referring to the pile of receipts and what-all beside it.

"Thought you were supposed to take it easy," he said. Casually. Focusing on the selection of sodas in the fridge and not on the ramped-up *hmmmmm* in his blood that happened every damn time he saw her.

"The incision's not in my head," she said, her eyes darting back and forth between the paperwork and the computer as she entered the figures. "And the laptop weighs half as much as Skye. So I'm good. By the way…Hunter's teacher called." She glanced up at him. "He told her you said you'd come perform for the kids in his class?"

"I did," he said, his cheeks warming as he popped the tab to the can.

"When did this happen?"

"While you were in the hospital. He asked me, and I said sure." He shrugged. "No biggee."

"It is for Hunter. Not to mention his class. She asked if sometime the week after next would work for you."

"I'll give her a call, we can work out the details. I've played for school kids before, Em," he said at her perplexed expression. "And…"

"And you miss being on stage," she said, teasing. "Admit it."

Cash dropped into the chair opposite, slouching, one ankle propped across his knee. Still casual. Like seeing those new-mother pouches under her eyes wasn't doing a number on his head. Like this whole freaking situation wasn't doing a number on his head. It was like his brain had split in two, the old It's-All-About-Cash Cash versus the new, marginally improved Cash. Both gave him the willies, but for entirely different reasons. Right now, it was not fun being him. Not that it ever had been, but still.

"I might," he said with another shrug. Although the truth was, teaching Hunter, goofing around with the guitar on the porch after supper all those nights…maybe things weren't as dead in that area as he'd thought. He'd even been working on a couple of songs, although he wasn't gonna tell her that. "Kinda hard to simply forget about something I've done for two-thirds of my life."

"I can imagine," she said mildly, returning to her task.

The foot over his knee began to twitch. "You want me to start dinner or anything?"

"In the slow cooker," she said, turning over a receipt. "Pot roast didn't weigh over ten pounds, either."

"Emma—"

"I have to keep going, Cash," she said quietly, not looking at him. "Mama left, you won't be around forever, no sense getting used to having people do for me."

Yeah, and weren't Cash 1 and Cash 2 having a grand old time with that one? "But the doctor said—"

"Not to overdo it." The computer shut, Emma finally looked at him, clearly exhausted. "I'm not going to do anything stupid, okay? But my life didn't go on hiatus because I had a baby."

Cash frowned at his soda can, then at her. "So if Lee was here, what would he be doing?"

Her eyes clouded a moment before a smile touched her lips. "Hovering. Fretting. Making me crazier than you are, most likely."

"Aside from that."

"Just…keeping on. Once everything's planted, it's mostly about waiting. Other than the greenhouse crops, there won't be much to harvest before mid-June. Goats need tending, of course—worming, hoof trimming. Can you do that?"

"Yes. But I meant in the house. With the baby. The kids. Would Lee bring you the baby at night? Change him?"

He saw her blink away tears before she nodded.

"I can do that."

From his seat, Skye screwed up his face and let out a sharp, startled wail. Emma glanced at the clock over the sink and sighed. "Every three hours, right on schedule. Come on," she said, pushing herself to her feet. "I've still got to lie down to feed him—"

"You go ahead and get yourself situated, I'll bring him."

As Emma carefully walked out of the kitchen, Cash unstrapped the now-frantic baby, curling him over his chest, high on his shoulder. But instead of relaxing, the baby only screamed harder, like he knew Cash didn't have what he wanted.

Yeah, that was the story of his life, wasn't it?

Emma had arranged herself on top of the covers on her bed, surrounded by about a million pillows. For a moment he pictured himself lying behind her, curved to her spine...

"You want me to change him?" he asked.

"Probably not. I usually do it between...at the halfway mark. Hand him over. No, don't go," she said, drawing the baby close. "Please. You can't see anything, I promise."

"That kinda takes all the fun out of it, doesn't it?" he feebly joked over a sudden shakiness in his gut.

"You are such a man, honestly," she said, then tilted her head sideways, indicating an old, comfortable armchair beside the bed. "Sit. Keep me company. Tell me about your exes."

"What?" Cash said, halfway down. "Why?"

"Because I'm bored out of my mind, for one thing. And for another I want to know how, not one, but two women could be stupid enough to let you get away."

Cash finally lowered himself completely into the chair, although the shakiness had escalated to an all-out earthquake. For a moment he listened to the muffled sounds of a hungry, nursing baby from underneath the little blanket Emma'd covered them both with, until he finally said, "I think it's more that they couldn't wait to get away from me. I really was a wreck back then," he said to her it-can't-be-that-bad expression. "Only thing I was good at was making bad decisions."

"Except about your career."

He almost laughed. "That was pure dumb luck."

"And talent."

Cash snorted. "God knows far more talented people than me never get anywhere. Or not very far, anyway. So I can't credit *choice* all that much, far as my career goes." *Or went,* he thought, then sighed, leaning back. "My wives, though… that's another issue entirely. The first one, especially—"

"Name?"

"Misty. For real," he said when she chuckled. "Anyway, I was twenty-one and about as full of myself as a person could get and not explode. Otherwise known as compensating for having no self-esteem. Or so the therapists said. Anyway, Misty was pretty and funny and made me feel ten feet tall. So I married her."

"That was it?"

"And you wonder why it didn't last," Cash said, warming to his subject. Oddly enough. "Basically we got bored with each other. And she wanted her own career, wasn't interested much in supporting mine. Can't say as I blame her, although the stars never lined up for her. Last I heard, she'd married a casino manager and moved to Vegas. We get in touch once in a blue moon, but…it's like her and me never happened."

"And Wife Number Two?"

"That would be Francine. I was all of twenty-six then. Older, but definitely not wiser." He mimed knocking back a drink. "She wasn't the least bit interested in being on stage, but she constantly nagged me about being away so much. Even though this wasn't exactly something I sprung on her, considering I met her on the road."

"She was a groupie?"

"Lord, no. Her daddy owned a music store in Dallas where I picked up some strings one day. She was pretty and funny and…" His cheeks creased. "Guess you could say there was a pattern there."

Emma smiled. "So what happened?"

"We fought. A lot. She wanted a kid. I didn't." He stared hard at the baby, wriggling underneath the blanket, and felt a pang. "The difference was, I *knew* why I didn't want a kid. Even setting aside how little I would've been around, I didn't much feel qualified to be anybody's daddy. Francine, though… I pretty much figured she wanted to be a mom so she'd have somebody to love her."

"She had you."

A humorless laugh scraped his throat. "What we had, was like some dry husk of a marriage. Looked okay on the outside, at least for a while, but on the inside? Nothing. Small wonder, since I sure as hell didn't have anything to bring to the table. So I wasn't all that surprised to get back from tour one Christmas Eve a couple years in to find a 'it's been a blast, see ya' note on the dining table, along with the keys to the condo. Said she was going back to Dallas, she didn't want to see or hear from me again."

"That's terrible."

"Actually, it was a relief." He let his gaze pierce hers. "Nothing worse than failing to live up to somebody else's expectations."

"She didn't want alimony?"

Cash smirked. "Apparently she already had Plan B in the wings. Seemed she hadn't exactly been pining away for me when I was on the road."

"Oh, Cash," Emma said gently, then lowered her eyes to the baby. She messed around underneath the blanket, then looked up. "If you bring me a diaper and wipes, I'll change him—"

"No, no…" He stood, almost too eagerly, to take the baby. Who thankfully smelled more of his mama's milk than what was in the diaper. "Don't tell me what to do," he said, setting him on the other side of the bed. "I can figure this out on my own."

"Go for it." Emma leaned her head in her hand, watching. And not saying anything, even though he used up six wipes to get the little butt clean. And an extra diaper since he had to slap the first one over the geyser that erupted before he'd finished.

"You might've warned me about that part," he said, handing her back the clean baby.

"And spoil my fun? No way." She'd gingerly sat up to nurse the kid on the other side, propping him on several pillows before looking at Cash again. "And there's been no one since?"

He should've known she wouldn't let go that easy.

"Not serious, no." Instead of sitting again, Cash leaned one hand on the footboard. "How come I can talk to you like I can't to anybody else?"

Her eyes grazed his. "Maybe because I *don't* expect anything from you."

"Maybe."

"He's asleep," she whispered a minute later, detaching the baby from her breast, which Cash caught a glimpse of, creamy in the muted light through the filmy curtains. "Would you mind putting him down…?"

"Not at all," Cash said, almost startled by how good it felt to hold the little guy, to feel all that innocent trust against his chest. He laid the baby on his back in the bassinet, watching him, stunned by the tiny, open mouth, the fat little cheeks and fisted hands. Emma came up beside him, her scent—*her* trust—turning him on more than he would've thought possible. Turning him inside out.

"He's Lee to a *T,* all right." At her silence, he turned, catching her conflicted expression. "Sorry—"

"No, it's okay," she whispered, touching the baby's head. Then, not looking at Cash: "Your second marriage…it ended about the time you decided to stop drinking?" At his silence, she gently added, "I was always good at math."

"You know that accident I told you about? It happened right after Francine left. Got mad, got drunk, got in my car. I thank my lucky stars every day it wasn't worse."

"You loved her, then?"

"The truth? I don't know as I've ever loved anybody the way other people mean the word. But I'd tried with Francine, as best I could. To be a decent husband, I mean. Yeah, I drank too much and was away too much, but…"

He crossed his arms. "There's a lot of temptation on the road. Plenty of opportunity to break promises. To yourself, to other people. And I'll admit when I was single, I might've taken advantage of some of those opportunities. Not all, but some. Never when I was married, though. So when Francine walked out…it was the failure that hurt like a sonuvabitch. That my best hadn't been good enough."

For once, it appeared Emma had nothing to say. Some bit of wisdom to impart. *Well, good,* Cash thought, turning to her, feeling that damn surge of tenderness again that was making his life hell. "You should really get some rest while he's asleep. You want me to get going on the laundry?"

"You know how to do laundry?"

"Since I was sixteen and realized it wasn't gonna magically do itself."

"Then have at it. And I think I will catch a nap," she said, carefully crawling back onto the bed to lie on her side.

Cash watched her until her breathing slowed, then quietly retrieved the laundry basket from her closet.

At least this, he couldn't screw up.

* * *

Not even on Open House night had Emma ever seen the school parking lot this crowded.

Hunter's teacher had called the day before, equal parts apologetic and apoplectic. Apparently, soon as word had gotten out about Cash performing for Hunter's class, the news snowballed, first through the school itself, then the rest of the village, until the teacher wondered if the school cafeteria would even be big enough to hold everybody. And she was *so* sorry since she knew this wasn't what Cash had intended. Not until Cash reassured her it didn't bother him at all did the poor woman calm down.

But now, seeing all these cars? Emma understood her initial panic.

"You sure you're okay with this?" she asked Cash as, with the starstruck janitor's help, he unloaded three guitars and an amp from the back of his car. Beside her, Annie kept up a nonstop conversation with a very awake Bruiser in his hand-me-down stroller as dozens of excited townspeople streamed into the squat, brick-faced building.

"More than okay," he said, hooking the case strap for one of the guitars over his shoulder, his whole demeanor radiating a sense of peace like she hadn't seen before. "Reminds me a bit of when I started out. All anybody had to say was, 'You know how to play that thing?' and I did." Then he stopped, looking at the building. "Wonder if it's changed any from when Lee and I went here?"

Emma smiled. "I doubt it."

"We can go in this way," Sal, the janitor, said, pointing to the cafeteria's outside door. Underneath opaque brown eyes and bushy, graying brows, a smile bloomed. "We already got a stage set up. Some lights, too. Left over from the Presidents' Day play."

"Couldn't ask for more than that," Cash said, then turned back to Emma, concern clearly warring with anticipation. "You sure *you're* up for this?"

And exactly how do you mean that? she wanted to say. Instead, she kept smiling. "I'm fine, Cash." Physically, anyway. She was healing up quickly enough to at least resume some of her work, even though it'd be a while before she was hauling fifty-pound feed sacks again. And Skye was even sleeping the occasional five-hour stretch at night now, *thank* You, Lord. So she was almost feeling human again. "Go on," she said, shooing him. "Do your thing. If you hear a catcall, that'll be Annie. I made her swear not to toss her panties up on the stage, though."

"Spoilsport," Annie grumbled, grinning, and Cash laughed. Yeah, he was one happy dude, all right.

"Good to know. See y'all later, then."

"Break a leg!" Emma called after him, because she'd heard that was what people said to performers before they went on stage. But Cash was already gone, yakking to Sal as they carted his equipment inside. Sighing, she fell in step with the hordes making their way toward the front door, Annie pushing the stroller, the old gal's recently permed curls a frothy white cloud around her face.

They found seats in the back of the hot, packed room where Emma could keep Skye in the stroller. Beside her, Annie chuckled as she fanned herself with some old church program she'd dug out of her white vinyl purse. "Fire marshal gets wind of this, we're all screwed."

"Annie!" Emma said, chuckling herself as Cash ambled out onto the small "stage," looking pretty darn good for a man who'd been up at night with the baby nearly as much as Emma these past couple of weeks. But in worn jeans, scuffed-up boots and a plaid shirt Emma'd seen a dozen times before, he looked no more like a "star" then she did.

Until he grinned and she saw the immediate, practically electric connection between him and the audience. Then she understood.

"Whoa!" he said, doing an exaggerated flinch for the benefit of the couple of hundred kids all sitting on the floor in front of the stage, earning him a chorus of giggles. "Where'd y'all come from?" More giggles. Then, pretending to frown, he propped his hands on his hips and scanned the crowd. "Hunter? Where are you, buddy?"

When Hunter yelled out, "Right here!" Cash pointed to him, then grabbed the mike off its base and grinned for the crowd again. "My good buddy Hunter here asked me to come for his class," he said into the mike, his low voice sending a chill through Emma. And probably every other female in the place. "Guess I forgot to tell him it was supposed to be a secret!" This said with a huge wink, and everybody laughed, and Emma could tell Cash was feeding off the attention and applause like it was his lifeblood.

Sal brought out a stool, which Cash grabbed and plopped in front of the mike, set close to the front of the stage. "You know," he said, scanning the electric guitars and amps set up behind him before, with a shrug, he chose the battered old acoustic he played on their porch. "All that stuff?" He arranged himself on the stool, one boot heel hooked over a front rung, the guitar in his lap. "Feels like overkill to me. Here, anyway."

One hand on his knee, the other one casually draped over the side of the guitar, he said, "Many of you might not know I grew up right around here. Well, partially, since I left home when I was sixteen. Which I do not recommend, by the way," he added, looking at the kids down front. "Went to this school, in fact. Hey, Miss Hutchinson—you still here?"

"I sure am!" came a clear, thin voice from the right, and everyone laughed again. "Except it's Mrs. Alvarez now."

His gaze directed to the middle-aged blonde leaning against the wall, Cash pressed a hand to his heart. "You didn't wait for me? I'm crushed, I truly am."

"You were six, Cash," the teacher said, laughing.

"Still old enough to know I'd scored the hottest first-grade teacher in New Mexico," he said, winking again for the audience. "Anyway—" he slapped the guitar "—let's do some music, how 'bout it? Any requests?"

For the next half hour, he played and sang like Emma imagined he must've done when he started out, relying on nothing but his clear, naturally deep voice accompanied by the mellow sound of an old acoustic guitar. More than once tears sprang to Emma's eyes as she listened, sometimes because of the music, more often because of the man singing it. At one point Annie reached over and wrapped her strong, wiry hand around Emma's, murmuring, "I know, child. I know."

Even so, the scales didn't tip entirely until, after the concert, Cash invited the kids to come up on the stage with him, first to join in singing some simple song he apparently made up on the spot, then to hold and touch and even play any of the guitars they liked. At one point Hunter whispered something into Cash's ear. Grabbing the acoustic, he nodded, then followed him down into the audience, to a severely disabled little girl in her wheelchair. Squatting beside the chair, Cash carefully set the guitar in her lap, then took her hand and slowly strummed her fingers across the strings.

Her verbal response was virtually unintelligible. But there was no misreading her dazzling smile. And when Cash looked up and caught Emma's eyes, an equally brilliant smile on his, an unseen force quietly opened the damper to her heart, letting the love pour out like there was no end to it.

Which, as it happened, there wasn't.

Chapter Ten

"To-day was the best day *ever*," Hunter said to Cash across the kitchen table that night. "I have a lot more friends now." He laughed his low nasal laugh, which earned him an indulgent, "Hunter, honestly!" from his mother.

"Me, too!" Zoey said, flashing a smile of her own. "You sound a heck of a lot better in person than you do on your CDs."

"Is that right?" To be honest, the buzz still hadn't worn off. To make that connection with an audience, any audience...no better high in the world. "So all that money I spent on fancy sound mixing and what-all—"

"Wasted," Zoey said, and Annie pressed her napkin to her mouth, smothering her laugh, and Cash glanced around the table, almost wishing—

"What'd you say this was again?" Annie said, jabbing a fork at the casserole Donna Garrett had donated to the cause that had languished in the freezer since Skye's birth.

"Not sure it has a name," Emma said, frowning as she prodded what was probably a piece of ham with her fork. "Best not to think about it too hard." Then her gaze lifted to Cash. "'Fess up—you had a blast today, didn't you?"

She'd been unusually quiet during the ride back to the house, like she'd worn herself out. Although she'd seemed fine when Cash returned from making deliveries to the two restaurants and three small inns Emma supplied with fresh produce. Now, though, he suspected a connection between her question and her earlier pensive mood. One that made him feel itchy inside.

"Not gonna lie," he said, forking in another bite of the mystery casserole. "It felt good, performing again. A lot better, in fact, than I'd expected."

"You were awesome," Zoey pronounced, nodding.

"Yeah," Hunter said, giving him a thumbs-up. "Awesome. May I be excused?"

"Me, too," Zoey said, dumping her napkin and sliding out of her seat before Emma gave her leave. "Granny—can we take Skye for a walk? It's still light out!" she said when her mother opened her mouth. "And warm! Just up to Veronica's. Please?"

"Yeah," Hunter said, the table shaking when he bumped the edge as he stood, too. "We can go see Ver-on-ica's kitties!"

"Veronica has kittens?" Annie said, out of her seat like a shot. "Why didn't somebody tell me? Zoey, get Skye changed, and Hunter, you get his stroller—"

"Don't you dare bring back another cat!" Emma said to Annie as she marched out of the kitchen through the writhing mass of cats they already had. After five minutes of the chaos involved with getting four people including a baby out the door, the house was empty and Emma hadn't moved.

"Em—?"

"Hear that?" she said, her eyes shut.

"I don't hear anything—"

"I know." She sighed. "Isn't it *wonderful?*"

Then she opened her eyes and Cash's gaze snagged in hers, and he thought, *Look away!* only he didn't know if he was talking to her or himself. Then Emma popped up from her chair to start clearing the table.

Whew, close. "Let me—"

"No, it's okay, I can do this much," she said, stacking the plates, pushing out an aggravated sigh when Cash took them from her and carried them to the counter.

"I don't get it," she said behind him.

He grabbed a tray and returned to the table for everything else. "Don't get what?"

"Why you think you're not good with kids. What you did today—that wasn't an act, Cash. That was real. That was *you.*"

Flushing, his gaze bounced off hers before he carted the tray to the counter. "Not like I was gonna be a jerk with all those people watching."

"You forget, I see you every day with my two. You've never treated them with anything but patience and kindness—"

"Yeah, well, it's no big deal being nice to somebody you know you won't be around long enough to screw up." He slammed open the now-fixed dishwasher and yanked out the bottom rack to start loading the plates. "Not my kids, not my responsibility."

He heard her walk over to stand beside him. "Maybe not," she said quietly, leaning one hand on the counter, the other on her hip. "But you're still not a jerk. And you're not gonna win that argument so you may as well give up now."

"*Damn* it, Emma!" Cash swiveled to meet her gaze, only to get so hung up in it he had no idea how to find his way out again. "You're driving me crazy, you know that?"

The words shimmered in the space between them for a moment before fading into the cushiony silence. Finally, Emma smiled, a *whatchagonnado?* curve to her lips that shoved Cash right over the line between *then* and *now*.

"Yeah. Same here." She hesitated, then lifted her hand to glide the backs of her knuckles down his cheek, and his breath curled into a hot, dry knot in the center of his chest. "Crazier than I've ever been in my life."

Emma saw Cash swallow, wanted to press her lips to those clenching muscles in his throat, to pull this man inside her—in more ways than one—so bad her own throat went dry.

"Shouldn't that be a bad thing?" he finally said.

"Don't know." She shrugged. "Don't really care."

His hand covered hers; she half expected him to remove it. To reject her, which she completely deserved. Heck, she didn't know herself why she was making a move destined to end badly. So her insides flipped when, instead, he gently turned her hand over to place a kiss in the center of her palm, making her suck in a sharp breath.

Once more his eyes grazed hers, a slight smile toying with his mouth. "You get turned on that easy?"

"It's a gift."

He chuckled, but there was a sadness about it that shattered her heart. "Just so there's no misinterpretation…you coming on to me?"

"Heh. Only as much as a woman who had major surgery three weeks ago can. The spirit's willing, but the body's probably not entirely on board with that idea for another three weeks or so."

Air rushed from his lungs before he pulled her into his arms, laying his cheek on her hair, and an untold number of tiny fire-tipped arrows launched in her stomach. "Just so there's no misinterpretation," she said into his chest, "this mean you're interested, or taking pity on me?"

His chuckle rumbled in her ear. "You're a lot of things, Emma, but pitiable isn't one of 'em."

She reared back to look at him. "Seriously?"

"Mmm-hmm." His eyes had gone thunderstorm gray. *Oh, my.* "But you don't strike me as somebody who messes around for the heck of it."

"I'm not."

His sigh warmed her mouth. "I don't want to hurt you, Em."

"Which is precisely why I'm not jumping your bones right now. Because I don't want to hurt me, either."

"No," he said on a dry chuckle. "That's not what I mean."

"I know what you mean." She slipped from his arms, forcing herself to find something to do, something mundane and real and unsexy. Like setting the table for the next morning. "I think that's called making light of the moment," she said, pulling bowls down from the cupboard.

Except she nearly dropped one when he slowly lifted her hair to place a lingering, tender kiss at the nape of her neck, the imprint of his lips still burning when he eased her around. She barely caught the apology in his eyes before his mouth touched hers, almost tentatively, like he wasn't sure he'd like the flavor. Then his hold tightened, his fingers tangling in her hair as he put some steam into the kiss, and her mouth opened under his, accepting. Welcoming.

Oh, honey, you're good, she thought as she sent her brain packing and let the kiss take over, let all that long-ignored need unfurl inside her, hot and sweet and hazy. If he touched her breasts, her milk would let down.

But he didn't. Instead he entwined their hands, bracing their linked fists on the counter on either side of her hips so that nothing touched but lips and tongues and teeth; he sucked her lower lip into his mouth, gently teasing, sending her hoo-hah into a tizzy.

Suddenly she laughed, and he looked at her, his eyes darkening even more with desire, confusion. "You're a whole lot of fun to make out with, Mr. Cochran," she said, and he gave her another one of those regretful grins.

"You, too," he whispered. "Long as you understand you're making out with a jerk."

"You're *not* a—"

"Shh," he said. Then moved closer.

A lot closer.

So close he had to hoist her up on the counter and wrap her legs around his hips so he wouldn't squish her.

Emma nearly went cross-eyed. "I take it you're real happy to see me," she said, and this time he laughed, and kissed her again, possibly the deepest, wettest, knee-knocking kiss she'd ever had in her life—which was going some, truth be told—pressing himself into her with clear intent, and her hoo-hah said, *Oh, yeah?* right about the time Emma realized, holy mackerel, they were in her *kitchen,* and then Cash pressed into her *just* a little harder and all hell broke loose down there.

Oh. Hmm. *Wee* doggies.

For a second, if that, she panicked, wondering if her recently C-sectioned innards were earthquake-worthy, but since they apparently were she figured *Oh, for pity's sake, relax and enjoy it.* Which she did.

A whooole lot.

When the room stopped spinning, she opened her eyes to see Cash grinning down at her. "You did that on purpose!"

"Yep. Had a sudden yen to see how you looked when you came apart." He swept her hair aside to have another go at her neck. She nearly swooned. "Didn't think you'd take offense, somehow," he murmured. Nibbling.

"Um…ah…n-no…"

On another soft laugh, he lifted his face. "You really don't hold anything back, do you?"

"What would be the point of that?"

Which apparently prompted some more tongue-tangling before Cash rested his forehead on hers. "Three weeks, you said?" She nodded. "You sure?"

"I'll have to check with the doctor, but—"

"No. You sure you want to do that again?"

"Um…yeah?"

"Naked?"

She laughed. "Oh, yes."

He paused. "With me?"

Man was gonna break her heart and that was no lie. She cupped his cheek. "Heck, yeah, with you."

"Even though—"

"Yes. Even though." Then she skimmed her thumb along his cheekbone and whispered, "You sure you want to stick around that long?"

"Something tells me it'll be more than worth the wait," he said, kissing her one last time before walking out of her kitchen. Which she would never think of in the same way again.

Twenty minutes later the gang returned, Zoey holding a new peach-colored kitten—"Don't get your panties in a wad, I'll pay to get him fixed!" Annie said—Skye fussing for his food. Feeling far too mellow to give Annie grief, Emma carried the baby into her bedroom, not surprised to discover her nursing pads were soaked when she put him to breast.

For several minutes she watched her baby boy chow down, waiting for the ramifications to hit. You know, those pesky things like guilt. Anxiety. Remorse.

Nada.

At least, not yet. Possibly because she was too busy basking in the afterglow for reality to get its foot in the door. That, and yearning for the man who'd produced that afterglow, which—not being born yesterday—she knew would come back to bite her in her ample butt.

When it did, she'd deal. But right now, with her mouth still tingling from Cash's kisses and her skin from his touch, his scent in her nostrils keeping that sweet ache pulsing in the pit of her belly…*later* seemed very far away.

Which was just fine with her.

Well, Emma thought, three weeks later as she stepped back into her jeans, smiling for Skye gumming his fist in his baby seat—here it was:

Later.

Moment of truth and all that.

"Everything looks great," Naomi Wilson said with a big smile. A dozen long braids, like chocolate licorice twists, swished against her white coat as she walked back to her desk in the no-frills office. "The incision's healed up nicely, and you say you're feeling pretty good?"

"Couldn't be better," Emma said, taking a seat across from the family doctor who'd been tending to the kids' boo-boos—and Emma's girl parts—for the past year or so.

"How long since the bleeding stopped?"

"Three, four weeks. So…I'm good for resuming, um, normal activity?"

A question which could have meant anything. Like lifting bushels of fruit. Or whatever. Except when Naomi's black eyes met Emma's, she blushed.

"Don't see why not," the doctor said calmly, looking back at Emma's chart. "Although you might want to...ease back into things. Take it slow and easy at first."

"Of course."

"Nothing too strenuous—"

"Got it, Naomi!"

Chuckling, the doctor looked up. "I'm happy for you, honey."

"That I can muck out the goat house on my own again?"

"Absolutely. Just make sure you have all the proper equipment before you do any of that...mucking. What is it, Rox?" she said with a smile to whoever had come to the door.

"Silas Garrett's out there, the color of a piece of Wonder Bread because his youngest boy fell and cut open his head. He said you were closer than the E.R.—"

"He still bleeding?" Naomi said, standing.

"It's bandaged, so I think it's stopped, but Silas says it probably needs stitches."

"Well, we'll see about that. Okay, Emma...you're good to go. Roxie, go ahead and schedule Skye for his two-month," she said, leading Emma back out front, passing a very distraught Garrett brother with a sniffing, bloodied four-year-old clinging so tightly to Silas he'd knocked his father's glasses askew.

"It's gonna be fine, Daddy," Naomi said, steering the pair down the hall. Roxie took a second to—Emma assumed—admire the view before easing herself behind the computer. She had to hand it to Donna and Gene Garrett—they sure did know how to make good-looking sons. If accountants had a male calendar, Silas would make one hot Mr. June.

"Why do parents always seem to take it harder than the kid?" Roxie said behind her.

Setting the baby down in his carrier, Emma smiled. "You have kids?"

The young woman paused, then shook her headful of dark ringlets. "Not yet," she said softly, focused on the computer. "When you do, you'll understand."

That got a brief smile as she brought up Emma's file. "Wonder how Mrs. Silas is going to take it?"

"Far as I know, the former Mrs. Silas flew the coop a couple of years ago."

Pale green eyes flew to Emma's, glittering with an odd mixture of humor and pain. "And the man is still single? Get out."

Not that Emma knew the particulars, exactly, but the gossip grapevine had long tendrils. "Not for want of candidates, from what I hear. And if they don't show up on their own, his mama goes out trolling for 'em. But when a man's been hurt…" She paused, thinking of Cash. "Sometimes those roots go deeper than can be dug out."

"Sounds like you're talking from experience."

"So," Emma said, pulling herself up short. "You're Naomi's new receptionist?"

"Only temporarily," Roxie said, her eyes on the computer screen. Her gaze flicked to Emma's, then back to the screen. "Came home to lick my wounds."

"From?"

"Kansas City. Although I doubt you're interested in my business. Two weeks from today at 10:00 a.m. okay?"

"Perfect. And clearly you've been away from Tierra Rosa too long," Emma said, and the young woman smiled. "A man?"

"A man. A job. My apartment." Roxie shrugged, then wrote out an appointment card and handed it to Emma. "So I figured I may as well help out Naomi while I pick up the pieces of my sorry life." She sighed. "Funny, how I always figured by thirty I'd have everything worked out. Not be back at square one."

Emma reached across the low partition to give Roxie's shoulder a supportive squeeze, declining to point out that Square One was the default setting for life. Which the gal would figure out on her own soon enough.

Skye had nodded off by the time Emma started home, giving her plenty of time to think. To ponder the foolishness of what she was about to do. Since she somehow doubted her womanly bits, as spectacular as they might be, had any magical healing powers to repair wounded souls.

She'd never had casual sex in her life. Didn't intend to now. She'd also never been in a situation where the give-and-take part of things wasn't equal…or where the potential to get her heart broken was so great. But without taking that risk, there was *no* chance of fixing Cash's, was there?

Emma checked her watch, figuring she had barely enough time to make a swing by the drugstore in the next town over to pick up some…equipment.

She might be crazy, but she wasn't an idiot.

Cash wrenched the ancient *acequia* spigot to the off position, then straightened to remove his hat, mopping sweat off his forehead with the hem of his T-shirt. His father had never used the Spanish colonial-era irrigation system which snaked through the property, as well as most of the northern part of the state, but Emma's vegetable fields were very grateful for the weekly allotment of water. The flooded fields glittered in the sun, serene and sated, as realization flooded Cash's consciousness that his reasons for hanging around were pretty much over.

That his services were no longer needed.

The other night, a beaming Emma had shown him her Quicken "books." God knew the farm would never make her rich, but she was once again in the black, especially since the state had finally agreed to pay off Lee's medical bills. And now that she had regular help again and Cash no longer had to take up the slack with the chores...

He slammed his hat back on and whistled for the dog, intending to return to the house for a glass of tea or lemonade. Except his plans were foiled when the old Suburban groaned into the driveway.

Emma's gaze barely glanced off his when she got out of the car and opened the door to get the baby. A light breeze tickled her loose, blue-and-white-striped shirt, her bra—her breasts— plainly visible underneath. Six weeks on, what baby weight she hadn't lost had regrouped into curves worthy of a forties pinup girl. There was nothing flat about her, anywhere.

Which was just fine with Cash.

"No, I'll get him," he said, not looking fully at her until he had the sleeping, dimple-kneed baby out of his car seat. For a half second he thought about leaning over to kiss her, like real couples did when they saw each other again.

Except they weren't a real couple. Would never be one. At least not in the sense that Emma would define the word. And, since fate had nixed any opportunity for funny business since that kiss three weeks before, they weren't even a couple in a way that Cash might define it, either.

Then he noticed how pink her cheeks were. Somehow he didn't think it was from the sun.

"What?" he said, shifting the sacked-out baby on his shoulder. Ignoring how naturally the little chunker molded to him. How good it felt.

Ostensibly watching the dog plod to the middle of the yard, where he collapsed with a groan, Emma blushed ever harder, then looked at Cash. "Got the all clear."

"To...? Oh. Well, hell. Nothing like getting right to the point."

"Didn't think you needed to be seduced."

"I suppose that's true enough." Palming the baby between the shoulders, he said, "Thought maybe you'd changed your mind."

"Nope. You?"

"Uh, no." Cash blew a short laugh through his nose. "So much for romance."

Emma busted out laughing, then covered her mouth when Skye jerked in his sleep. "Romance," she whispered, "is for people who don't have to deal with a house full of people who watch your every move."

Also true. And yet…something was bugging him about this. Took him until they were back in the house and she'd laid the baby down in his crib before he put his finger on it. "You don't think you deserve romance?"

She spun around, her hands still hovering over the baby, then shooed him back down the hall to the kitchen, Annie's megadecibel TV amply covering their conversation. "What I think," she said, going to the fridge and pouring both of them tumblers of sweet tea, "is that this thing between us is…" Frowning, she sipped her tea, then said, "More honest than that. It is what it is."

Cash leaned against the counter. Chugged half of his own tea. "And what's that?" he said over the roar of canned applause in the other room. The even louder roar of lust in his veins.

"Another step in your recovery process."

His brows shot up. Then down. "I know you're nuts—which is okay, nuts is what I like about you—but if you think I want to—" he lowered his voice "—sleep with you as part of some exorcism ritual…that's not nuts, it's flat-out insane."

Unperturbed, she took another sip of tea. "Then what would you call it?"

"I don't know. I don't go around trying to define everything like you do. What's wrong with wanting to make love to you because I *like* you?"

"Nothing. Nothing at all. But then, there's nothing *romantic* about that, is there?"

Cash blew out a sigh. "Put that way...I suppose not." He finished off his tea, then said, "So what's your reason?"

"Does it matter?" she said softly, her gaze pinned to his, and a pleasant heat bloomed in parts south. A pleasant heat that was going to become extremely *un*pleasant if they didn't do something about it before too much longer. "Not that I have any idea how we're going to pull this off, exactly."

"Leave it to me," he said, and she grinned, then left the room, all those curves gently swaying underneath her soft, clingy shirt.

The man was a genius.

"Your mama's been cooped up in this house with your baby brother for six solid weeks," Cash said the next evening at dinner. "So I'm taking her to Santa Fe to see a movie. That okay with you, Annie?"

"Sure thing," she said, blotting her mouth with her napkin and slipping tidbits under the table to who knew how many cats. "The baby's going for four hours between feeds now, so why not? I'll call Jewel, see if she wants to come over and watch a movie or something—"

"Already done," Cash said. With a straight face.

"Then we're set. Go out, kick up your heels! Live!"

Don't look at Cash, don't look—

When Emma stood to clear the table, Zoey twisted in her chair. "How come we can't go?"

"Because," Emma said, returning to the table, "it's a grown-up movie."

"With cussing and naked people?"

"Zoey! Honestly!"

"Maybe," Cash said.

"Eww!"

Emma scooted—for real, these days—to the counter with the next load of dishes, blushing so hard she felt feverish.

"Can we stay up un-til you get back?" Hunter asked as she heard Cash's chair scrape across the floor.

"No," he said, coming up behind her, close enough for their respective pheromones to dosey-do and her nipples to go *Ten-hut!* "I'll get this," he murmured, "you go feed the baby." As she fled down the hall, she heard him say, "If we're not back by nine-thirty, you two go on to bed…"

As soon as Jewel arrived—bearing videos and popcorn—they were on the road, headed toward Cash's mountain house, Emma with enough butterflies in her stomach to repopulate the entire Amazon Rainforest.

"If you're thinking of backing out?" Cash said softly beside her. "It's okay, I half want to catch that new Matt Damon flick, anyway."

Finally, the laugh she'd been holding in for the past hour escaped. "You do not."

"Well, yeah, I do," he said, then grinned over at her. "At some point."

"I'm not backing out, Cash. It's just feels so…" She lifted one hand, let it drop. "Planned. Unromantic."

"Is that one of those female-logic things?"

"Yes," she said, and he chuckled.

"Then pretend it's not. Pretend…" He reached over, took her hand. Started making circles in the center of her palm with his middle finger. Hel-*lo,* erogenous zone. "Pretend we really were going to the movies, only while we were waiting on the popcorn our hands touched and we got so hot we ran back out of the lobby like a pair of idiots—"

"Were people staring at us?"

"You bet. Overcome with envy, most of 'em. Since it was pretty obvious what was going through our heads. So anyway, we left the movies—" he let go of her hand to navigate a curve in the road "—and now we're on our way back to my place, our hearts pounding in anticipation of the night of wild lovemaking ahead of us. What's so funny?" he said, his grin far brighter than the setting sun slicing through his window. And oh, my, did she love that grin.

"You are," she said over her own chuckle, then sighed, looking out the window. "Seems a shame, though. Forfeiting our tickets like that."

"We gave them to that pair of teenagers, remember?"

"Oh, right. I forgot." She looked at his profile, half wishing she knew what he was really thinking. "Thanks."

"No problem."

A few minutes later, they were inside his house. Her first impression was that there was nothing wrong with it, exactly, but…

"There's nothing of you here, is there?"

"Same as every other place I've ever lived," Cash said, unlocking the dining room's patio door. "Guess you have to know who you are for that to happen." He slid the door open, gesturing for her to step out on the deck. "View's terrific, though."

Emma braced her palms on the wood railing to take in the village below, the endless, slate-colored mountains in the distance. A breeze danced across her cheeks, soothing and arousing all at once, then plucked at her loose hair, blowing it into her face. Shoving it back, she smiled, then turned to see Cash watching her, his expression thoughtful. Tender. Aroused.

"What?"

"You are so damn beautiful it almost hurts to look at you."

She laughed. "Get out."

"I'm serious. Thought it the minute we met. And about a million times since. Lee struck gold with you, and that's a fact."

"Wow," she said, her eyes burning. "You're smooth."

"Come here," he said, his voice a little shaky—or that might have been the breeze in her ears—and she went, sighing into the kiss as he wrapped her in his arms, and it felt good and right and ten kinds of wrong at the same time, which was thrilling since she wasn't a ten-kinds-of-wrong kind of girl.

Eventually, he led her into the bedroom, where Eli Garrett's magnificently carved headboard momentarily took her breath, a room suffused with the heady, masculine scent of clean linen and aftershave and oiled leather from the half-dozen pairs of boots soldiered along the wall. They undressed each other between unhurried kisses and soft laughter—over stubborn buttons, feet tangling in jean bottoms—until there was nothing between them except the breeze lazily spilling through the open window, the final, piercing rays of the setting sun, their own gazes.

Emma reveled in Cash's thorough appraisal. She loved her body, her breasts that had nourished three babies—and were no longer leaking, praise be—her wide hips that had borne them, even the folds and stretch marks they'd left behind. It had served her well, this body. Judging from Cash's expression, it would soon serve him well, too.

Smiling, she closed the gap between them, the sunlight embracing them both.

If the woman hadn't made her move when she did, Cash might've stood glued to the spot for God knew how long, stunned stupid.

They'd progressed to the bed, lying facing each other, nothing touching but their eyes. Not what he'd expected. Emma, either, most likely. With any other woman, all that eye contact would've unnerved him, made him feel vulnerable. And he wasn't sure that was not was happening here. The difference was, he didn't care. The difference was, he trusted Emma enough to *be* vulnerable.

Which was what was so unnerving.

When the explorations finally got under way, nobody was in a rush. Cash spent a long time simply fiddling with her hair, sifting it through his fingers, coiling it around his palm and letting it go. Grazing the ends across one pale, marbled breast, then flicking it across the nipple. He watched, fascinated, as it hardened, like he'd never seen anything so amazing in his life.

Emma crooked her elbow to prop her head in her hand. "Can't remember the last time I felt this appreciated. It's nice."

Cash mirrored her position. "Will you let me live if I said there's a lot to appreciate?"

She laughed, then stroked a finger across his shoulder, making him shiver. "Somehow I figured we'd be going at it like rabbits by now. That we're not is a real pleasant surprise."

"You like foreplay, then?"

"My second favorite part. But I swear, the way you look at me…that alone's enough to make me fall apart."

"Yeah?" She nodded, all that trust in her eyes, and he felt like he was being crushed inside. He caught her free hand, held it tight against his chest. "I can't promise you anything."

"Then it's a good thing I don't expect you to," she said, suddenly shifting to push him on his back.

"What are you—"

"Shh," she said, her hair cascading over them both as she straddled him, then slowly, deliberately skimmed her fingers over his shoulders and down his arms, across his collarbone, his pecs. She curled forward to lick first one nipple, then the other, murmuring, "Let me have my fun."

"This gonna get kinky?"

Her teeth flashed in the semidarkness. "Probably not. But if you ask me, anybody who thinks plain vanilla is boring has never tasted real—"

Her tongue swirled around one nipple, then the other.

"—rich—"

She sat up to trail one finger to his navel.

"—creamy—"

And farther down, only to slowly drift back up before she got to where all the troops had amassed, eagerly awaiting orders to storm the valley.

"—full-bodied vanilla. 'Cause I'm here to tell you," she said softly, tossing her hair over her shoulders so the flickering shadows from the live oaks outside trembled over her breasts, "there's nothing better in the world than vanilla done right. Now hush and let me love you."

So he hushed, except for the occasional hiss and moan, letting her touch and taste and explore to her heart's content, her mouth and hands a damn miracle, soft and hot, gentle and generous, until she took him into her mouth and everything blurred into one big fiery ball of want, and then he felt her roll on a condom, carefully lower herself until he filled her, and her breath escaped her parted lips on a long, satisfied "Ohhh."

Then everything stilled as their eyes locked again, absorbing the moment, absorbing each other, and Cash tensed, fending off Emma's attempts to breach his barricades, to reach inside and tug free his emotions. No, he thought, bracing himself against her pull, refusing to let his defenses crumble, knowing the moment he let her in he'd be helpless as an infant.

Holy hell, it's never been like this scuttled through Cash's brain before he tentatively moved inside her, afraid to hurt her. Afraid, period. Of the helplessness. Of the feelings surging inside him, desperate to find the way out.

No! sounded even louder in his brain as he clamped his hands on her waist and pulled her tighter against him, retaking control—of her, himself, the moment—only to feel everything sway again when her eyes drifted closed and her breathing hitched, releasing on a sweet moan…as he felt his heart—the heart he'd sworn didn't exist—shift along a hairline fault he would've sworn didn't exist, either.

And she smiled, victorious.

NO, dammit! he thought, pushing up even higher inside her, and this time she matched his thrust, gasping at her first spasm, and slow and gentle evaporated as she gave and gave and gave, more and more and more with each wave until they swept him away with her, and he dimly remembered somebody telling him the French called this the Little Death. Now he knew why.

And when it was over, he checked to make sure his heart, although cracked, was still locked up nice and tight. From what he could tell, it was.

But damn, had that been a close call or what?

Far more rattled than she wanted to let on, Emma kissed Cash and got out of bed, where it took her three tries to get her trembling arms through her shirtsleeves.

"Where you going?"

"I just need…" The shirt barely buttoned, she yanked her hair out of the collar. "It's okay, I'll be back."

She'd intended to go out on the deck, but got sidetracked by what was apparently his music studio. There wasn't much in the cinnamon-walled room—an old, small dining table, a couple of chairs, a dozen guitars on stands lining the walls.

But once inside she noticed the pad of paper and mechanical pencil on the table, a half-filled mug, the coffee cold and disgusting. She angled her head, saw what were obviously the words to a song, half of them crossed out, rewritten, crossed out again.

"When did you do this?" she asked when she heard Cash behind her, standing in the doorway.

"I've been coming back here now and again for the past couple of weeks. At night, usually. When I couldn't sleep. Em—you okay?"

She turned. He'd pulled his jeans back on but hadn't buttoned the top button. Seeing him stand there, his thumbs hooked around the loops, tugging them below what most folks would consider decent, was enough to get her hot and bothered all over again.

The concern in his eyes, the gentle set to his mouth, though, turned her heart inside out. And that was far worse.

"I'm fine," she said, shoving her tangled hair out of her face. "But you don't strike me as a cuddler."

His eyes narrowing, he leaned against the door frame, scratched the back of his neck, then crossed his arms. "What is it they say, about not being able to kid a kidder? Same goes for BS. I'm the king, Emma. Or so all the shrinks said. Emotionally defensive, I think is the term for it. You thinking about Lee?"

"What? No! No," she repeated on a breath. "Which maybe surprised me a little, that I didn't. That was…" She crossed to the keyboard, skimming her fingers along the keys. "A little more intense than I expected."

He was quiet for a second or two, then said, "No surprise considering the way you make love."

"So you're writing again," she said, nodding toward the pad. Changing the subject. "That's good."

After a long pause, he said, "Just an idea I wanted to get down. I get lots of ideas. Most of 'em never turn into actual songs." He walked over, wrapping her in his arms from behind. And oh, it felt good, to feel taken care of, even if only for a little while. Even if it was only pretend. "Guess I miss it more'n I wanted to admit."

You knew going in this wasn't about miracles.

You knew.

"We should probably be getting back," she murmured, pulling away, except he held fast, his mouth hot behind her ear as he deftly unbuttoned her shirt, then took the weight of her full, heavy breasts in his hands, and she sighed, happy. Content, despite the stinging in her eyes.

"We have an hour, yet," he murmured, his touch scorching her skin, melting her resolve, making her laugh when he added, "I ever tell you vanilla's my favorite flavor?"

Chapter Eleven

"So how was the movie?" Annie asked the next morning as Cash sat at the kitchen table, glowering at his half-drunk cup of coffee. A herd of cats followed her, meowing for food.

"Fine."

The old woman tossed him a glance, hmmphed and went to refill two of the three continuous feeders. "Care to talk about it?" she asked over the whoosh of kibble against plastic.

"No."

Swiping kibble dust off her front, Annie shuffled to the coffeemaker for her own cup, then plunked down across from him. "Not talking about the movie."

"Neither am I."

"You fixing to leave?"

Cash's eyes lifted to hers, dropped again. "Can't see much reason to stay. Emma's back on her feet, the farm's in pretty good shape, I can be in the house without wanting to throw up. So there's one chapter finished. On to the next."

"You got any idea what that is?"

"Workin' on it."

"You ever consider maybe the next chapter is here, too?"

"Not even for a second." Which was a bold-faced lie, because he'd thought about nothing else since he'd brought Emma home less than twelve hours ago. Except every time he tried to visualize himself sitting at this table twenty years, five, even a month down the road, the picture kept coming up blank.

"She loves you, you know."

Cash flinched. "Don't say that."

"I'm old, I can say anything I damn well please." Then, with an you're-an-idiot look, Annie pushed herself up and left him to stew in his own juices.

The irony, of course, was that he felt closer to Emma than anybody he'd ever met. Still, he had no doubt that, given enough time, even the unflappable Miss Emma would find herself seriously contemplating taking a two-by-four to the side of his head. Hell, he'd already seen frustration flash across her face a few times, even though she'd done her best to squelch it. He just had that effect on people. Only most of 'em didn't bother trying to hide it.

Not that he wouldn't miss her. And the kids. And all the rest of it. But she needed a man who could be as generous with himself as she'd been with him. Not somebody who'd deliberately held back at the very moment when she'd given him everything she had. And then some.

Twice.

Punching out a rough sigh, Cash got up for a fresh cup of coffee. His cell rang; he frowned at the readout, contemplated letting it go to voice mail, then answered anyway, his manager cutting off his "Yeah?" with, "So you are still alive. Good to know."

"What do you want, Al?"

"For starters? For you to get your ass back to Nashville and start working again."

"Noted. Next?"

The older man laughed. Al Parrish had been a two-bit nobody until he'd heard Cash perform at some equally two-bit honky-tonk sixteen years ago, along with a dozen other yahoos biding their time until Lady Luck bit 'em in the butt. In Cash's case, Lady Luck was a balding, chunky little man with dubious taste in jewelry and mysterious family ties to half the Nashville music scene. Like Cash, Al'd been waiting for his big break—in this case, somebody with that indefinable *something,* as Al put it, that would put them both on the map.

At twenty, Cash would've signed his life over to the devil himself for a shot at the big-time. What Al hadn't realized was that it'd been more the other way around. Precious few other managers would've put up with his crap during those early years. But Al's main talent lay in his ability to either ignore or look past the stupidity. In fact, he'd come as close as anybody to really believing in Cash. Except for—

"Francine called last week, looking for you."

"What did you say?"

"Francine—"

"Never mind, I heard you. What on earth does she want?"

"To talk to you?"

"Tell me you didn't give her my number."

"I'm not an idiot, Cash. She did say it was urgent, though."

Cash swept The Black One off the counter. Cat gave him a wounded look and stalked away. "She sound okay?"

"She sounded like Francine. Take that any way you like. You want *her* number?"

"No. But give it to me, anyway." Cash scanned the counter for something to write with, found one of Zoey's markers, scribbled the number on a napkin. "That all?"

A moment passed before Al said, "You not even working on any new songs, nothing?"

The tug was a lot harder than he'd expected, an ache, almost, to crawl back inside what he knew, even though what he knew didn't really exist anymore. "I might be. For my own amusement. Why?"

"Cash, nothing would make me happier than if you'd end this little hiatus and get back on stage. Start recording again. You're still young, for cripes' sake, what's to say you can't reinvent yourself—?"

"And piss off the few fans I have left? Why on earth would I do that?"

Al sighed. They'd had this conversation a dozen times in the past year. "You've got a lot more than a few fans left—"

"For how long? Look, you know I'm not interested unless I can headline. And only if I can do what I'm good at. Be who I am." On stage, at least. "Not some 'reinvented' version of myself. Nothing sadder than a has-been reduced to opening for some young stud twenty years younger than him."

"What makes you think I can't get you a headline booking?"

"Can you?" A challenge, not a plea.

"Maybe. Probably. Sure, let me see what I can work out—"

"Al. Don't."

"But if I could. On your terms. Would you come back?"

Cash stared outside, at the sunflowers headed toward eight feet tall, the apple trees heavy with new fruit. Sunflowers he'd planted. Trees he'd pruned. None of which were his. "Maybe," he said at last, and Al breathed out a sigh. "Not making any promises, Al. Just...exploring possibilities."

"Cash, you gotta trust me, your career's far from dead—"

"I'll let you know. Talk to you soon."

He turned to find Emma watching him, the baby sacked out in the funny sling she wore when she went about her chores. One brow rose, as close as she came to prying.

"That was Al. My manager."

"So I gathered."

"How much did you hear?"

"Nothing I wouldn't have expected."

"We weren't talking about anything definite—"

Her laugh cut him off. "Cash, I'm not blind. Or stupid."

He rubbed his jaw, then shoved his fingers into his front pockets. "Country music…it's changed. I'm not even sure…" His head wagged. "But it's what I know, Em. What I'm good at. The one thing I apparently can't screw up."

One hand cupping the baby's head, Emma went to the fridge for a bottle of juice. Automatically Cash took it from her to twist off the top, feeling his forehead pinch.

"If you're expecting me to try to talk you out of leaving," she said, nodding her thanks when he handed her back the open bottle, "you've got a long wait. Not my style. Besides, like I said, it's not a surprise—"

"No, it's not that, it's…" He exhaled, his head already feeling crowded without wondering why Emma's giving up so easily was ticking him off. He should be grateful, right? He met that steady gaze and thought, *Yeah. Gonna miss you bad.* "The main reason Al called was because Francine's looking to get in touch with me."

The juice halfway to her mouth, Emma paused. His picking up his career again had been bound to happen eventually, even if she wasn't feeling as copacetic about that as she was letting on. She sure hadn't counted on an ex reappearing in his life, though. Neither had Cash, apparently, judging from his expression. "You're kidding? After all this time?"

"Yeah," he blew out. He held up the napkin, the bright turquoise numbers bleeding into the soft paper. "Her number."

"So call."

"And say what?"

She knew the question was rhetorical, that he wasn't so much asking for her input as he was sorting through his options. Which was as it should be. After all, this had nothing to do with her.

"I'm sure you'll think of something," Emma said, realizing her heart was breaking, dagnab it. So she carted the baby and her juice outside to check on the kids in their new, expanded pen. Not so much because they needed checking up on, but because she needed to absorb some of their unbridled joy. She had so, so much to be grateful for, it was downright petty to feel cheated about not getting the one thing she'd known all along she couldn't have. Because "having" Cash wasn't possible. Not only for her, for anybody.

Didn't make it any easier to let go, though. Especially since she hadn't realized how tightly she'd been holding on.

Hearing Cash's slow footsteps behind her, she turned, only to start at the devastation on his face. "Cash...what is it—?"

He walked over to the fence, clasping the top. Emma gave him his minute while he apparently processed whatever he'd just heard. When he finally spoke, his voice was strained.

"I've got a son."

"What?"

He emptied his lungs, then looked over. Shock, disbelief, anger were all tangled up in his eyes, making her heart break a little more. "He's seven. Francine was apparently pregnant when she left me."

"Ohmigosh…Cash." Whether he wanted it or not, she covered one of his hands with her own. To her surprise he grabbed hold and held fast. "But…how can you be sure?"

"She said if I don't believe her I can certainly have a DNA test done when I get there."

"So she's going to let you see him?"

At that, a harsh, pained laugh pushed from his chest. "Oh, I can do you one better than that. It seems the guy she left me for? When he found out Wesley wasn't his, he split. And Francine's not exactly wild about being a single mother. So she's decided…" He squeezed her hand harder. "She wants me to take him."

"*Take* him?" she said, thinking, *Yeah, here's where that seeing-everybody-as-God's-child thing gets a little dicey.* "As in, simply hand him over after not even telling you about him? That's rich."

"One way of putting it."

"So…are you going to?"

"Hell, Emma—I don't know!" He pushed away from the fence to pace in front of it. "I only found out about him ten minutes ago! Have no idea if he even knows about me yet." He turned, his face contorted. "*Damn* it—he's a little kid! How's he supposed to go from his mother to some stranger like it's no big deal?"

Spinning around, he grabbed the fence once more, bowing over it for a second before shoving off again, backing away. "I gotta…I need to get out of here, figure out what I'm supposed to do next."

Except, as Emma watched Cash stride to his SUV and get in, she knew exactly what Cash would do, even if he didn't.

Because for all commitment scared the bejabbers out of him, the man she'd gotten to know over the past two months would, without doubt, put the needs of a little boy whose life was about to be turned upside down ahead of anything else. His own needs. His career. And certainly *way* ahead of a relationship that had barely gotten started.

A fact she saw clear as day when his gaze touched hers before he drove off.

It took Cash three days before his head cleared enough to face Emma again. Three days of long drives and sleepless nights, of inner battles the likes of which he'd never known, of forcing himself to make the hardest decisions he'd ever made.

Wearing a body-skimming top nearly the same color as her eyes, she was rocking the sleepy baby on the porch glider when he drove up, her gaze questioning but calm as he got out of the car.

"Wasn't sure if I'd see you again," she said quietly when he came up the steps.

"I was hardly gonna head out without saying goodbye," he said, thinking any other woman would've given him hell for leaving her in the dark that long. That she didn't, that she wouldn't... For the hundredth time, it hit him she was the only gal he'd probably ever regret leaving. He bent to pet the dog. "You alone?"

"Kids are still in school, Annie's at art class. So, yeah. Just me and Bruiser, holding down the fort. Can I get you something?"

His stomach heaved. "For God's sake, this isn't... It's not a social call."

"No reason to throw common courtesy out the window." She stood, then squatted to put the baby in his bouncy seat, and Cash stared at them both, miserable. "When are you leaving?"

"Tomorrow. Early."

Straightening, Emma picked up a glass of something from the wicker table beside the glider and took a sip, lifting the hem of the shirt to hook her thumb in her belt loop. "You selling the house, then?"

"Don't know yet. Not sure what I need it for, but Tess thought I should hold off until things were more settled. Which makes her the only Realtor in the state who'd turn *down* a listing."

Her lips curved. "Is there a plan?"

"At this point? Not really. I don't even know what Francine's told Wesley. If he has any idea what's about to happen. Although…" Cash waited out the pang. "I'm gonna try my best to talk her out of giving him up."

Emma's eyes narrowed. "Really."

"Not for the reason you think," he said, almost mad. "Not for me. But because I can't see how it would be good for the kid."

"Depends on the situation, I suppose." She set the drink back on the table, adding softly, "Children know when they're not wanted."

"Tell me about it."

Her gaze still steady, still threatening to suck him back in, she frowned, like she wasn't sure she should say what she was thinking. "Before you go, you need to know something."

"And what might that be?"

"That this is your home, Cash. Always will be. Wherever life leads you, whatever you decide to do…" She patted the porch railing. "This is here, waiting for you."

"No, Emma, the house is yours, fair and square—"

"I'm not talking about the house, I'm talking about family. Belonging. I know, it's crazy, and if you'd asked me two months ago whether I'd even be thinking in terms of letting another man into my life, into my kids' lives—"

"You're right, it is crazy," he said, wanting this conversation to die. Now. "About as crazy at it gets. Because I don't *belong* anywhere."

"And what makes you so all-fired sure about that?"

"Because..." He glanced away, dodging that infuriatingly calm gaze. "I didn't know what to expect when I came back here. Didn't even know what I was looking for. The missing pieces to who I was, I suppose—"

"And did you find them?"

He looked back. "I don't know. Not yet. But I told you up front I didn't want to get involved, didn't want to be 'part of the family.' Okay, maybe I saw a chance to make a difference in somebody's life in a way I never had before, but for damn sure I didn't expect..."

The words wilted in his throat.

"To bond?" Emma finished for him.

Cash crossed to the other side of the porch, leaning hard on the railing, watching, against the endless sky, the piñons sway in the lilac-scented breeze. "Dammit, Emma—being here it's like getting sucked into a dream. A dream where I'm pretending to be somebody else. As nice at it is, it's still a dream. And dreams end. Always."

At her silence, he looked over his shoulder to see her watching Skye, her tender gaze on her son sending pain shooting through him.

"In my head," he said through a tight throat, "I get what happened with my father. That it had nothing to do with me. But like I said, the scars go deep. Real deep. No, listen," he said when she opened her mouth. "Honey...I've screwed up every relationship I've ever had. I don't know why, or how, but I do. I mean, come on—doesn't it tell you something that my ex didn't even see fit to tell me I had a son until now?"

"Yeah. That she's an idiot."

A dry laugh shot from his mouth. "You don't think anybody's an idiot."

"I'll make an exception in this case," she said, walking toward him, her arms folded across her ribs. "There's no way you would've messed up your relationship with your own child, I don't care what you were going through at the time."

"You don't know that."

"Says the man who's turning his *own* life on its head for a child he's never met. Yep, you're gonna make a lousy father, all right."

Cash blew out an exasperated breath. "Taking the obvious first steps doesn't mean the rest of it will fall into place. That we'll hit it off. Or hell, even like each other."

"Oh, for heaven's sake…he's *seven,* Cash! If the way Hunter and Zoey took to you is any indication, I doubt his liking you is going to be an issue—"

"Depends on what his mother's told him about me, doesn't it?"

"Man, do you know how to set up roadblocks for yourself or what?"

"Better than setting myself up for disappointment."

Releasing a breathy, humorless laugh, Emma shook her head. "Okay…I'm just gonna say this. Maybe a couple of months isn't much in the scheme of things, but it's long enough to convince me that the Cash I know? Isn't the Cash you've convinced yourself you are."

"Emma, don't—"

"No, let me finish. Since you're leaving anyway, it's not like I've got anything to lose. It's not that you don't belong anywhere, Cash, it's that you don't *believe* you do. Big difference. I said you had a home here, and I meant it. Will always mean it. But as long as you hang on to the belief that you don't—or that you're not really good, or worthy of having somebody love you—nothing I or anybody else can say or do is gonna convince you otherwise. You're the only one who can fix you. Which isn't gonna happen until you're ready to be fixed."

As a thunderstorm of emotions pelted him, she closed the space between them to lift a hand to his face, all that honesty and goodness in her eyes likely to tear him to pieces. "The man who writes those songs that used to turn me into a blubbering mess…nobody can fake those feelings. Just like there was nothing fake about what went on between us the other night. But you gotta love yourself, honey, before you can feel anybody else's love." Her forehead creased, she soothed a thumb over his cheek. "Like mine."

Cash felt like all the air had been siphoned out of his lungs. "You don't love me, Emma."

"Oh? Says who?"

"Me. Because you're too smart to love something that doesn't exist, to love somebody who's only—"

"A stand-in for Lee? You're right, I am. But then, since I never, not once, thought of you as a substitute for my dead husband, that's your problem, not mine. I love *you,* not Lee's memory. So deal."

Furious, confused, Cash swept past her and down the porch steps, nearly to the car when she called after him.

"Just promise me one thing."

Against his better judgment, he turned back. "And what's that?"

"That you'll try. With your boy."

Their gazes battled it out for a long moment before, with a sharp nod, he got in his car and drove off.

Away from something he should've never let himself get tangled up with to begin with.

Emma was still doing the catatonic thing on her porch when, an hour after Cash left, Noah Garrett drove up in his supermacho truck, an event which prompted Bumble to lift his head in mild curiosity and Emma to realize the emotions she'd kept a lid on from the moment Cash showed up were backed up in her throat, ready to erupt.

Almost like he understood he needed to tread carefully, the young man tentatively approached, muscles on full display underneath the black T-shirt tucked into his camouflage carpenter pants.

"Afternoon," he said with a nod. Afraid to speak, Emma nodded back. Noah licked his lips. "Uh…Cash left a message? That I needed to set a time with you when we could start the remodel?"

"I'm sorry," she got out before snatching up the baby and hoofing it back into the house, where the slam of the screen door behind her probably didn't muffle her sobbing one tiny bit.

Chapter Twelve

As many times as Cash had played Dallas, he didn't know the city at all. So even with his GPS system it took a while to find Francine's house, tucked deep in a suburb north of the city proper. Place looked decent enough, he supposed, at least from the outside. Typical brick-façade, ranch-style house, live oak in the grassy front yard. Kid's bike lying on its side on what passed for a porch.

Cash had to force himself to breathe. His first Super Bowl halftime gig hadn't made him feel this close to puking. Unfortunately, no more an option now than it had been then.

The white, scrolled-iron screen door swung open before he was halfway up the walk. "You made good time," Francine said, unsmiling. She didn't look a whole lot different, except for maybe being a mite heavier. Still the same shaggy blond hair, fake tan and perfect makeup, the same preference for shrink-wrapped clothing—in this case white shorts and a blue top that showed more than a sliver of midriff. Still pretty, to be honest.

Long as you didn't scratch too deep below the surface.

"Go on in. Wesley's down the street with a friend, I'll go get him."

When she passed, her flip-flops slapping against the cement walk and her perfume about to choke him, it struck Cash how much he dwarfed her. He'd forgotten, how often he'd taken up with small gals who'd giggle and tell him how big and strong he was.

Hell.

Once inside, he glanced around the dimly lit living room, the shades drawn against the summer heat even though air-conditioning purred through the vents. Like Francine, the place was neat. Orderly. Devoid of clutter. And animal hair, he thought with a tight smile, remembering she was allergic—

"We're back," she announced, making Cash jump. He turned, breath frozen in his lungs as he laid eyes on his son for the first time. The boy stared back, slate-blue eyes steady underneath a grown-out buzzcut that, along with the too-big front teeth, made him look a bit like a hamster. "This here's your daddy, honey," Francine said, and Cash heard the nerves in her voice. His eyes swung to hers—was she having second thoughts? But like she'd read his mind, she shook her head, then said, "This is Wesley. Well, go on, honey—say hi."

Shrinking farther into his mother, the boy shook his head, confusion puckering his brow. "You're not my daddy. Daddy went away for a little bit, but he'll be b-back," he said, his bravado no match for his quivering chin.

And in that instant, the crack Emma'd left in his heart opened a little more.

Only this time, there was no closing it back up. No keeping out the fear, the helplessness. The sense that another person held your happiness in his hands. His big, scared eyes.

That, likewise, you held his happiness in yours. Because, despite the nearly crushing terror that comes from suddenly confronting your worst fear, Cash instantly knew nothing else mattered except this little boy.

Nothing.

"I told you, honey," Francine said, "Danny's not coming back. I know you don't want to hear that, but it's true."

Tears overflowing dark lower lashes, Wesley shook his head, his quiet, "No," filling Cash with something close to rage.

His heart thundering, he crouched in front of his son, barely able to get out, "It's nice to meet you, Wesley," past his knotted throat.

The boy jerked away and ran to the patio door, bouncing it open before streaking into the backyard. Calmly, Francine walked over, closed it again. "He'll be okay. Soon as he has a minute to get used to the idea."

"He needs a helluva lot more than a minute! For God's sake, Francine—how can you even think about dumping him?"

She spun around, her mouth open. "You're his father! How is that *dumping* him?"

"What else would you call handing him over to a complete stranger?"

Huffing out a breath, his ex dropped onto the blue-and-beige tweed sofa, her head in her hands. "Because I suck at being a mom, okay? It wasn't so bad when…before Danny left, but…"

She sprang back up, heading into the open kitchen to mess around with something on the stove. "Wes isn't a bad kid, I know that, but…it's like I have no patience with him. Every little thing he does sets me off. I know I yell at him too much.

And now that it's just us, it's only going to get worse. I can't quit work, so I'm exhausted when I get home, and here's this kid who needs me." She turned, apology in her eyes. "I'm no good at being needed, Cash. No good at all. Which you know."

"So what was all that about wanting a kid when we were married?"

"You're mad."

"Damn straight I'm mad!" Cash's pointed finger jabbed toward the door. "He's not a pair of shoes that don't fit! He's your *child*—!"

"I didn't know it would be like this, okay? That it would be so...hard." She faced the stove again, rattling the lid back on the pot. "I'm sorry!"

Frustration and red-hot fury roared through Cash, egging him dangerously close to a line he'd sworn never, ever to cross. Struggling for control, he snapped his head toward the kitchen window to watch a crouching Wesley poke at something with a stick.

My son, he thought, and the anger flared, crested...began to retreat. "Look...the kid's obviously well cared for, so I doubt you're nearly as bad as you think you are." *Heh. Sound familiar?* Ignoring the voice, Cash looked over at her. "Maybe you could take some parenting classes. Or if it's money issues stressing you out, I'll give you whatever you need so you wouldn't have to work—"

"Babe, you're not getting it. I don't want to be around him *more*."

"Holy hell, Francine," Cash said on a drained sigh. How had he spent three years of his life with this woman? "Do you even love him?"

To his shock, she teared up. "In my own messed-up way, I think so, yeah. Which is why I want you to take him."

"Even though you didn't see fit to tell me about him before this."

Shrugging, she fiddled with the wooden spoon. "I was mad at you. Stupid mad. And I thought Danny would give me something you wouldn't. Or couldn't. I swear I didn't know I was pregnant when I left." Her mouth pulled tight. "Then, when I found out, I honestly didn't know if you or Danny was the father. Although I guess I suspected it was you all along."

"And exactly when did it occur to you to find out for sure?"

The spoon abandoned, Francine combed her fingers through her hair. "I didn't. I mean, I was going to, but..." She sighed. "The truth is, things've been weird between Danny and me for some time. About six months ago he started going on about how he didn't think Wes was even his. So when I was at work one day he took him and had a DNA test done."

"And I should believe you, why?"

After a moment's stare, she pushed past him to the living room, where she pulled an envelope out of a desk drawer. A second later, she smacked it into Cash's hand. He glanced at the papers inside, then said, "This only proves Danny isn't Wesley's father."

"I know. But I swear you and Danny were the only possibilities. Although feel free to check yourself if you don't believe me. Yeah, I cheated on you. But I'm not a tramp."

No way was he going anywhere near there. "You even consider how your...decision might damage the kid?"

"And I'm telling you he'd suffer a lot worse if he stayed with me. Okay, I suppose it'll hurt for the moment, but in the long run...trust me. This is better. He'll get over it. Get over me. Besides, like I keep saying...stranger or no, you're still his father."

Although God knew logic had never been Francine's strong suit, this was prize-winning even for her. "You walked out on *me,* remember? So what makes you think I'd make a better parent than you—?"

The patio door crashed open again and Wesley stormed back into the house, flushed from the heat, only to come to a dead stop when he saw Cash, like he'd forgotten he was there. Immediately he looked to Francine.

"C'n I play in the sprinkler?"

"Sure, go get your swimming trunks on," she said, and he barreled down the hall, yelling at the top of his lungs. Francine winced. "Lord, *why* don't kids come with volume control?"

Even though Emma had virtually said the same thing about her own, there'd been love and good humor cushioning her words, whereas Cash could only hear acid in Francine's. Enough to provoke a bad taste in the back of his throat.

"Fine. I get it. But cutting you out of his life entirely…not gonna happen. And don't even think about arguing or I will turn around and walk out of this house."

Fear bloomed in her eyes. "You wouldn't."

True. But she didn't know that. "I let you go without a fight, didn't I? So I'm thinking you might not want to chance it."

His trunks on, Wesley caromed back down the hall and out the patio doors. A second later water shot ten feet into the air from the sprinkler and Wesley shrieked in feigned shock.

"So what're you proposing?" Francine asked at last.

"First off, I'll get a suite or apartment or something close by so I can come over every day until Wesley gets used to me. Until he trusts me—"

"You'd stay in Dallas?"

The very question that'd plagued him since he'd found out about Wesley. Damn, this whole thing was like putting together a puzzle without the picture. One piece at a time was all he could commit to. "If I have to."

"But…what about your *career?*"

Sidestepping the jibe, he said, "This is all about Wesley, Francy. Not you, not me. Wesley. When he's ready, and only when he's ready, then I'll take him by myself—"

"Meaning, when *you're* ready?"

Leaning one wrist on the edge of the counter, Cash said softly, "You've got some nerve trying to lay a guilt trip on *me.*"

Francine blinked, then frowned. "You've changed."

He almost smiled. "That good or bad?"

"I haven't decided," she said, turning back to the stove. "But I suppose you may as well stay for dinner. The sooner we get this get-acquainted business started, the better. I still can't cook worth crap, but I haven't killed anybody yet."

Letting her get on with it, Cash returned to the window, watching the boy. Oh, yeah, he'd changed, all right.

In ways that were scaring the hell out of him.

"Have you even heard from Cash since he left?" Jewel asked over the roofers' blunted, off-sync hammering as she loaded a bushel of cabbages onto the back of Lee's old pickup, parked between the fields. By July Emma was not above commandeering any bodies she could find to get the first major wave of crops harvested; fortunately, both Jewel and Patrice were totally on board with exchanging a few hours of manual labor for fresh fruits and veggies.

"No," Emma said in a low voice, cradling the baby in his sling while keeping one eye on Hunter some twenty or so feet away as he methodically picked green beans, inspecting each one before he put it in his basket. Zoey was off with Patrice, picking strawberries. Both kids had been mopey as all get-out after Cash first left, so Emma'd resorted to hours of hard labor to wear them out too much to think about it. After all, if it worked for her, why not her kids?

Except it didn't work all that well for her, either.

In fact, she still thought about him nearly constantly, even after a month. Wondered about him, how he was getting on with his son. If he was still in Dallas. If she'd ever see him again, when she was in a particularly masochistic mood.

"Oh." Jewel's broad-brimmed hat flopping lazily around her sweaty face, she grabbed a bottle of water out of the cooler beside the truck and twisted off the cap. With no makeup and in her capris and ruffly little top, she didn't look much older than Zoey. "I'm sorry. I would've thought…" She grimaced. "I'll shut up now."

The baby awakened, wanting a snack. Emma shimmied backward onto the lowered tailgate to get him out of the sling and put him to breast. "It's okay. It does get easier the more I talk about it."

"Really?"

"No."

"Oh, good. Not that you're hurting," Jewel quickly added. "But it's good to know you're not some paragon of woman-hood the rest of us have no hope of ever living up to."

Emma softly chuckled. "I'm hardly that."

"It sure seems that way sometimes," the young gal said, wriggling her much smaller hiney up beside Emma, wincing when she touched a hot spot. "The way you handle everything with such…grace. I mean, seriously—Cash had that whole heartbreaker aura going on, you know? Just like that one over there," she said, not really hiding her grin as she took another sip of water.

Emma followed the younger woman's gaze to see Noah saunter into view, checking on how things were going.

"Something tells me," she said, "you're here a lot more for the view than you are to help me harvest my vegetables."

"I am not!" Jewel said, blushing, her smile giving her completely away.

"But if you know he's a heartbreaker, why—?"

"Because I wouldn't give him my heart to break," Jewel said, shrugging, and for a moment Emma half wished she was a sure-footed twenty-five-year-old again, convinced she could will the world—and her heart—to do her bidding. Then self-pity, envy's first cousin, tramped on through, making her question how she'd managed to fall in love with yet another man who'd left her, even if Lee hadn't exactly had a say in the matter. Two hurts like this in as many years seemed patently unfair, somehow.

At that very moment, though, Skye swatted at her breast, and she looked down, and he let go of the nipple to gurgle at her and bat his big, dark blue eyes before latching on again with a contented baby sigh, and Zoey appeared, grinning, her hands and face stained red, lugging a flat of sweet, luscious strawberries from Emma's own patch, and she thought, *Oh, for pity's sake...look how much you* have!

Kids and friends and family and baby goats and things growing from the earth and endless sky... She shut her eyes, ignoring the prickle of longing that would try to derail her contentment, sending up a little prayer that Cash might one day find even a little of that peace and contentment, wherever life took him.

Letting Skye clasp her finger, Emma thought about how the joy gained from loving Lee, then Cash, far outweighed the sting of losing them. The hard part was accepting that she really couldn't have saved Cash, any more than she could have Lee. That fixing Cash had never been her job. Just like she'd told Zoey, Cash was simply one of those people who had to work things out on his own, and in his own time. Still, she liked to think that maybe, just maybe, Cash had left with a little more than he'd arrived with.

That her love had somehow blessed him, as it had her, even if he had no idea what to do with it.

* * *

"And this," Cash said, "is your room whenever you stay over."

Although he'd been in Dallas nearly a month, hung out with Francine and Wesley for some part of every day, they'd never been to his hotel suite until now. Francine had tried to back out, naturally, until Cash pointed out that Wes was far less likely to balk at sleeping over if she came with him the first time. She'd grudgingly agreed, taking her car, too, so Cash wouldn't have to run them home afterward. The minute they arrived, though, she escaped onto the small patio looking down on the hotel's pool, where she'd been ever since.

Wes looked up at him, suspicion still tensing his tiny shoulders. "Stay over?"

"Yeah. Whenever you want. The whole weekend, even."

"But…none of my stuff's here."

There was nothing much of Cash's, either, except his clothes and his instruments. Everything else was still in New Mexico. Still in limbo, just like him. "You can bring over whatever you want. We'll even take down those dumb paintings and put up posters, whatever. And see? There's two beds, if you want to have a friend come spend the night. We can go swimming, too—"

The boy gave him a *Dude, take it down a notch* look, then turned and walked past him to the suite's living room, efficiently furnished in Marriott Modern. For the moment the place was more than adequate, spacious and convenient to Francine's. Something more permanent would come later, after the next step presented itself. Besides, Cash didn't want to overwhelm the kid with "stuff" or make him want to be with Cash for the wrong reasons.

In any case, Wesley already had every game system ever invented, his own flat-screen TV and designer clothes that clearly meant nothing to him. "Stuff," he had. What he didn't have was the very thing that had eluded Cash his entire life. Whether Cash could provide that, he still had no idea. But he'd sure give it his best shot.

"I thought we'd order pizza," he said, returning to the living room. "How's that sound?"

The kid's head snapped around, his eyes wide. "I'm staying here *tonight?*"

"If you want, sure. But it's entirely up to you."

He shook his head as Francine came back inside, her smile as bright as it was insincere. Even Cash had to concede she truly was out of her depth with the boy, that what came so naturally to Emma had missed Francine entirely. What was far more painful, though, was how much Wesley craved his mother's affection. Same way Cash had his father's.

"What a great place, Wes, huh? Won't it be fun to spend the night here?"

The boy zinged a look at Cash, shrugged, then crumpled into a corner of the blue-green sofa, his sneakered feet not touching the ground. "There's no yard."

"But there's a pool!" Francine said. "Besides, I'm sure this is only temporary? Right, Cash?"

"Absolutely. You up for pizza?"

"Um, sure, sounds great. Hey," she said, slip-slapping across the carpet, "why don't I run to the store and get some ice cream to go with that?"

Wesley shot to his feet, stumbling over the carpet to get to her. "Can I come, too?"

"No, sweetie, not this time. But how about I stop by the house to get your swimming trunks so you can take a dip in that pool?"

"Okay, I guess."

"There's my good boy," she said, bending over to cup the back of his neck and kiss his hair before slipping out the door with a little wave. "You be good for Cash, okay? I won't be long."

As Wes ran to the front window and watched her drive off, panic speared through Cash. *Just try,* he heard Emma say.

Try.

"Uh…you wanna watch TV or something?"

His nose pressed up to the window, still watching, Wes shook his head.

"Then I guess I'll call for that pizza. What do you want on it?"

"Just cheese. Please."

As Cash dialed, he saw Wes crane his head, shifting his whole body weight until he practically fell over. "Whatcha looking at?"

"Somebody walking a dog." He shoved away from the window, dragged himself to the couch and bellywopped onto it, kicking one leg. "Can you have a dog here?"

"I don't know… Hello, yeah, I need to order a large supreme and a small cheese, bread sticks and…" He glanced over, wanting so hard to do right by this kid he could hardly breathe. "You like wings?" Wes nodded, cheek smushed into the sofa cushion. Cash added wings, gave his address and phone number and hung up. Now alternating legs as he kicked, the boy stared at him.

"Mama showed me one of your CDs. You're famous, huh?"

Feeling like his nerves were gonna eat him up inside, Cash walked over to drop into the chair perpendicular to the couch. "Depends on who you ask. I don't feel famous, though."

"What do you feel?"

Cash shrugged. "Like an ordinary person, I s'pose."

Wesley pushed himself up, grabbing a small throw pillow. Tucking his legs underneath him to sit cross-legged, he began lightly punching the pillow, over and over. "How come I didn't know about you?"

Apparently as antsy as his son, Cash got up, going into the kitchenette to pull down the stack of paper plates and napkins from the cabinet. "I suppose the same reason I didn't know about you. Nobody told me."

Not surprisingly, the boy bounced up again to wander into the kitchen, opening the mostly empty cabinets and slamming them shut, then skimming his fingers along the counter's edge before grabbing the end to hurtle himself into the living room, where he plunked facedown on the carpet. Cash stepped over him to get to the dining area, where he set out the paper goods. Behind him, he heard Wesley flop over.

"Mama says it drives her nuts, that I'm always moving."

"That's what seven-year-old boys do. It's okay."

"She doesn't understand."

"Women don't." Most women, anyway.

"Daddy didn't either." It took a moment to realize he'd said Daddy, not Danny. Another moment to swat the sting away. "How long's Mama been gone?"

"Five minutes, maybe?" Which Cash knew because he'd just checked his watch.

"Oh."

The kid was on his feet again, slogging over to the sofa where he perched on the edge. Picked up the remote. Turned the TV on. Zipped through a half-dozen channels, turned it off again. Sighing, he got up and pinballed his way down the short hall to "his" room, and Cash realized keeping him in the suite for more than ten minutes was gonna drive them both around the bend. He thought of Emma's frolicking baby goats and smiled, now understanding why small children were called "kids."

"Cash?"

"Yeah?"

"C'n I pick whichever bed I want? I mean, you know. If I decide I wanna stay over."

"Knock yourself out. Sh…oot, I forgot to order sodas. What do you like, I'll call your mom and ask her to pick some up."

"Dr. Pepper." Cash heard a muted thump. "Oh, wow. This bed is *awesome*."

Was that a giggle? Okay, maybe this won't be so bad after all, Cash thought with another smile as he punched in Francine's number.

Except the smile died when the ringing switched to a recording, telling him Francine's cell phone number was no longer in service.

Chapter Thirteen

As the days ticked by, Cash lost count of the times he'd almost called Emma. To ask—hell, beg—advice. To glean some of that serenity. To hear her laugh. Man, he would've killed to hear her laugh.

Except every time he was tempted to dial her number, reason—or stubbornness, he wasn't sure which—prevailed. That this was his problem to solve and nobody else's, a problem he couldn't run away from or leave for someone else to clean up.

Not that this revelation made things any easier.

He'd read Wes the note that'd arrived, along with his clothes and toys, three days after Francine's vanishing act. Part of it, anyway. As brutal as it was—about how she figured the only way to wean him away from her was to make a clean break, go where he couldn't see her—he didn't figure Wesley needed to hear the part about how she'd been seeing someone who didn't want kids.

Either.

During the two weeks since, Cash had alternately given the kid his space and pried him out of the suite "for his own good," hauling him to every attraction, every kid's movie, every amusement venue Dallas had to offer. He'd encouraged him to talk, to go swimming, to invite his friends over. He'd eaten hamburgers and macaroni and cheese until they came out his ears. He'd tried hugging him, only to be rebuffed every time. He even looked up a child therapist for Wesley to talk to, but he wouldn't talk. Hell, Cash had even prayed, on the off chance somebody was listening.

Nobody could say he wasn't trying. Wasn't still trying, he thought as he looked at the boy, slouched on the sofa playing a video game. His heart ached with wanting to make it better. To fix it. But how did you fix someone who didn't want to be fixed?

Welcome to my world, he heard Emma say in his head.

Not exactly what he meant by wanting to hear her voice.

"Hey, pork chop, it's a nice evening. How about we go ride our bikes?"

Wesley shook his head. "Mama might call."

Sighing, Cash scraped the bottom of his mental barrel for the last scraps of patience. "She's not going to call, buddy."

"She could change her mind, you know. Women do that."

Cash smiled despite himself. "Well, I've got my cell, if she does. And you need to get out, work off some of these bad feelings. Me, too. So come on. We can go get ice cream afterward, if you want."

"I don't want ice cream. Or to go bike riding. I want Mama."

"I know you do," Cash said, frustration boiling over inside him, "but that's the one thing I can't give you! So just drop it, okay?"

Hurt blue eyes collided with his. Crap.

"Wes—"

"Boy, it must've made you *real* mad when Mama dumped me on you."

Sure the top of his head would blow off, Cash plunked his butt on the coffee table in front of his son and wrapped his hands around Wes's skinny calves.

"And if that's what you think," he said steadily, "then I'm doing a worse job of this fathering thing than I thought. You bet I was mad your mother dumped you. Seeing-red mad. Because she hurt *you*. Not because she left you with *me*. That, I'm not at all sorry about. Not one bit."

A tiny crease dug between Wes's brows. "Really?"

"Cross my heart." Then Cash released a long breath. "I am sorry, though, that I yelled earlier. That was wrong."

"S'okay," Wes said, looking back at the TV. "Mama yells a lot, too. I'm kinda used to it."

Oh, brother. "Maybe so. But that's wrong, too. Sure, people get mad at each other, or frustrated, or whatever, but there's ways of getting the point across without yelling." He hesitated. "My father used to yell at me all the time. I hated it."

For the first time, the kid looked at him with a glimmer of interest. "You didn't like your daddy?"

"Actually I loved him, when I was little. Until I realized how mean he was to me and my brothers. My mother, too. But...but mostly to me."

"Like, how?"

"He smacked me around a lot, for one thing," he said softly. "I was always bruised, always hurting. Worse, though, was how he'd tell me I was stupid, that I'd never amount to anything. He even broke my first guitar, just because...well, I never really figured out why. I found out later—a lot later—that he had a problem in here—" Cash tapped his temple "—that made him act like that. But I didn't know it at the time. It kinda messed me up, too. When it came to knowing how to act around other people, I mean. Probably one reason why your mama and I couldn't stay married. I don't suppose I was a real good husband. And it's why…"

He hesitated, wondering how honest you should be with a seven-year-old. "It's why I didn't think I wanted kids, either. Which is also why I'm guessing your mama didn't tell me about you. Because she thought I wouldn't care. Or want you. She was real wrong about that. Even if I didn't know how wrong…" Squeezing Wes's knees, he said through a thick throat, "Until I met you."

"Yeah?"

"Yeah." Cash leaned forward till they were practically nose to nose. "You're one of the best things that's ever happened to me, Wes, and that's no lie."

Wesley looked back at the TV for several seconds, then slipped off the sofa and into Cash's arms, hugging him hard… and the instant Cash realized he'd put out his own eye rather than willingly hurt his son, or violate the trust he hadn't even yet earned, a light broke through, illuminating his own father's pain when he discovered what he'd done. What he'd lost.

Why he'd cried when he'd heard Cash's CD.

Cash held Wes closer, his eyes shut against the light, the understanding, but there was no stopping it now, as it banished every last shadow, burned out those roots of unworthiness and inadequacy and resentment and, yeah, even the hate, and tears stung, that what Emma had said was true, about it being all in his head. A lie, when you got down to it, fed to him by a sick man…a lie that had been in Cash's power all along to debunk.

A *lie* that had never truly touched who he really was.

Exhaling, Cash released his son, only to clamp his hands around his arms and look right in his eyes. "I'm gonna make a home for you, Wes. Haven't figured out the details yet, and I'll probably make a ton of mistakes—and feel free to tell me when I'm screwing up, I won't take offense—but I can promise you I'll do my best. From now on, it's you and me."

The kid's face puckered for a moment before he asked, "What if Mama decides she wants me back?"

"Too late. I might be persuaded to share, but damned if I'll give you up now. Although I guess I'm not supposed to cuss around you, huh?"

"Not like I haven't heard it before," Wes said with an eye roll, then laid his hands on Cash's shoulders, his gaze earnest. "You know, I think this is gonna work out okay."

Cash smiled. "Yeah. Me, too."

"So…can we go ride bikes now?"

"You bet—"

"Except there's one more thing."

"What's that?"

"When you said 'you and me'…you meant that, right? *Just* you and me? No girlfriends or anything?"

"Not a problem," Cash said, even though, suddenly and profoundly, it was. Because letting himself fall for his son had apparently crowbarred that crack in his heart full open. Allowing him not to only see, and accept, those first glimmers of forgiveness for his father, but for Emma to tumble right inside.

Yeah, there was irony for you. To finally fall in love, only he couldn't do a damn thing about it.

Because for the first time in his life Cash understood why people put their kids' needs ahead of their own. Even he knew he and Wes still needed time to figure out who they were together. That their relationship was far too new and fragile to introduce a whole other family into the mix. Besides which, for damn sure Emma didn't need another kid to mother. No, she didn't.

So that was that, he thought as they toted their bikes downstairs and set off for their ride in the waning light. Wes's exuberant, joyful yell as they coasted down a hill? That was worth any sacrifice.

At least, that was his story and he was sticking to it.

For Wes's sake.

"'Lo?"

Zoey froze, Mama's cell phone clamped tight in her sweaty palm. As it was Mama'd have kittens if she knew Zoey was calling Cash, but she just knew if *he* knew how sad Mama was he'd come back. But she hadn't expected some kid to answer. Maybe she had the wrong number?

"Um…I'm looking for Cash? Cash Cochran?"

"That's my dad. He's in the shower. Who's this?"

Oh, right. Mama'd said Cash had a little boy he'd never met before. Guess this was him.

"My name's Zoey Manning," she said, sounding all grown-up. "I'm a friend of your daddy's. He stayed here with my mama and brothers and grandma and me this summer. On our farm in New Mexico."

"Mexico?"

"*New* Mexico. Between Arizona and Texas. What's your name?"

"Wesley. But everybody calls me Wes. You live on a farm?"

"Yep. How old you are?"

"Seven."

"I'm six. Well, almost seven. In two months. We have baby goats. Ten of 'em. They're real cute but they make some real stinky messes which Hunter—that's my big brother, I've got another one named Skye but he's a baby—and I have to clean up."

"That sounds disgusting."

"It is. Almost as bad as the messes the baby makes in his diaper."

"You got any other animals?"

"No. Well, a *ginormous* dog, and Granny has about a million cats, but that's it. Hey," she said, getting a bright idea, "you should tell your daddy to bring you here for a visit sometime. If your mama'll let you come, I mean."

It got quiet for a while before Wes said, "Mama left. We don't know where she is. So it's just me and Daddy. But anyway, I don't think we could come 'cause Daddy says we're moving to Nashville next week and—"

"Wes? Who on earth are you talking to?"

Hearing Cash's voice, Zoey nearly slapped down the phone right then. But before she could, she heard Wes say, "Some girl named Zoey, she said you stayed at her farm?" and then Cash's voice was in her ear, saying, "Zoey? Is everything all right, honey?"

"Oh, um…yeah, everything's fine, I just—" She took a deep breath. "Mama misses you, I know she does, she's been listening to your CDs, the ones Daddy used to play? And she's never done that before. We all miss you, and Hunter needs a new song to play before he drives us all *nuts* with 'On Top of Spaghetti,' and, and…" She thought. "And Skye's gotten real big, he smiles all the time now, and Noah and them finally got Granny's new rooms finished and—"

"Zoey? Who on earth are you talking to?"

"Uh…the phone rang and I answered it for you," she said, practically throwing the phone at Mama and running. But not too far.

"Hello?" her mother said, and when Zoey saw her face, she knew she'd done the right thing. Even if she knew Mama'd have a few choice words to say when she got off the phone.

"Emma?"

Oh, Lord. Hearing Cash's voice in her head was one thing; hearing it for real was a hundred kinds of bad. She cleared her throat. "Zoey said you called me?"

"Um…no, actually. She called me. Well, actually she and Wesley have been having quite the conversation."

Emma sent an I-am-so-gonna-get-you-for-this glare at her unrepentant daughter, clinging to the door frame to hear what she could hear. "I see."

"You do? Because I sure as heck don't."

"It's about little girls sticking their cute little noses where they don't belong." Then they both said, "How are you?" at the same time.

"You first," Cash said, then added, in a low voice, like maybe somebody was in the room he didn't want to overhear, "Damn, it's good to hear you, Em," and that sturdy rope tied so tightly around her self-control these past few weeks began to unknot like somebody'd greased it.

"We're all doing good," she said, sounding perky as all get-out. Brother. "Baby's growing like a weed. The kids, too. The goat kind, I mean. Hunter just got back from that camp I was telling you about. He had a blast. Weather's been about perfect since you left so the crops are happy, the addition's finished…" Tears crept into her eyes, anyway. "Ohmigosh, Cash—I can't tell you how happy Annie is with her new digs. Thank you. Thank you so much."

"You're welcome."

"Oh! And I'm buying ten acres off our neighbors to the south, they don't need it and the goats do. They gave me real good terms. The neighbors, I mean. Not the goats." She knuckled a tear off her cheek. "And you? How's the boy? He look like you? You work things out with your ex about custody?"

And only *about custody, because if you say you worked things out otherwise I will have to kill myself. Or you. Somebody.*

"Wes is great, I don't know if he looks like me or not, and Francine took herself out of the picture."

Emma sank onto the kitchen chair. "You're not serious."

"A few weeks ago, yep. Said she'll get in touch when she's ready. We've got her new cell number, but she won't tell us where she is."

"Ohmigosh, Cash…" At least now she knew who to kill. One dilemma solved. "How's the little guy taking it?"

She heard the whoosh of a patio door opening, the distant drone of what sounded like a plane. "About as well as can be expected. Although truthfully I think it was more about having what he knew yanked away from him than anything. Not that I'm trying to paint Francine as some evil person, because she isn't—"

"Um, Cash? Abandoning your child ranks right up there. Sorry."

"True. But I honestly think she'd been doing her best. Only her best wasn't so good. Anyway, it gets a little better each day. Between Wes and me, I mean." He paused. "I went ahead and told Tess to put the Tierra Rosa house on the market. Since I won't be needing it."

That dull thud was the sound of her stomach free-falling. "You're moving back to Nashville."

"No reason to stay in Dallas. And Wes needs to get settled before school starts. Man…never thought I'd see the day when my life revolved around a kid's school schedule." He paused. "When my life revolved around a kid."

She could hear the amazement, and fear, in his voice. "How's it feel?" she gently asked, even though she already knew the answer.

"Like somebody else moved into my body." She laughed, even as a second tear trickled down her cheek. "Em?"

"Y-yeah?"

"I want you to know…if it hadn't been for you, I'd be a mess right now. No, I swear," he said when she laughed again. "Before I met you I thought unconditional love was a crock. That nobody loves without wanting something in return. But the more I get to know my son, the more I understand what that means."

She smiled, swiping at that tear. "Kids do that."

"Maybe. Except…except you showed me how it's done. You…" He hauled in a breath. "Dammit, Em—being around you all those weeks…it opened me up. Made me feel. Whether I wanted to or not."

"Scary, isn't it?"

"As hell. But…it's freeing, too." He chuckled. "You should also probably know that whenever I hit one of those what-do-I-do-now? patches with Wes, I ask myself how you'd handle it."

"You don't."

"Yes, ma'am, I sure do. And most of the time I get a pretty good answer. At least, the kid hasn't run away or reported me to the authorities or anything."

"You goof. But you know, all that you're feeling? It was there inside you all along—"

"I know," he said quietly. "That's what I finally figured out. You planted the seed, Em, and I guess being around Wes—well, he's either the sunlight or the water, I haven't quite figured out which. But I don't hate myself anymore." She heard him clear his throat. "Or my father."

"Oh, Cash…" Her eyes flooded. "I'm so glad."

"*You're* glad?" he said on a rough laugh. "Took me half a lifetime, but it's over. I'm free. Whoa—is that Skye crying?"

"You mean the tornado siren?" she said, beyond grateful for her child getting her off this phone before she turned into a blubbering fool. "Because, you know, I never feed him."

"Won't keep you, then," he said, laughing softly. "Great talking to you, Em."

"S-same here. You take care, okay? And, hey—let me know when you get to Nashville!"

Emma hung up practically before he said goodbye, too full of emotion to even fuss at the girlchild responsible for her mutilated heart.

Cash shoved aside the patio door and stepped back inside, his head ringing. Because even before Emma hung up, he realized...well, hell—if he'd spent half his life trying to figure out where he belonged, what earthly sense did it make to walk away, now that he'd found it?

He looked at Wes, AKA the fly in that particular ointment, who was sitting with his arms crossed, staring at the TV. Which wasn't on.

"Mama's not coming back, is she?" he asked. Not sadly, though. More like...resigned.

Cash closed the patio door, leaving his fingers curled around the handle as he shook his head. "Highly doubtful."

"You don't want really to go to Nashville, either, do you?"

His brows crashed. "What makes you say that?"

"'Cause your smile looks all fake every time you talk about us living there."

A huge breath left Cash's lungs as he crossed to the sofa beside his boy, his hands clasped between his knees. "Not really. Not to live, at least. I'm not the same person now I was when I lived there before. It would kinda feel like…taking a step backward."

"I know what you mean," Wes said, nodding sagely. He twisted on the couch, his face crumpled. "So what do you think we should do?"

Pile our crap in the SUV and head west at the earliest opportunity?

He slid his arm around Wes's shoulders and tugged him to his side. "You know the girl you were talking to? And her mom, who I was talking to?" Wes nodded. "They live in the house I grew up in. A place that had a lot of bad memories for me—"

"Because of your dad?"

"Yeah. So I went back there a couple months ago to see…" He faced the boy. "To face down the bad stuff, prove to myself the memories couldn't hurt me anymore."

"Like a bad dream?"

"In a way, yes."

"Did it work?"

"Sort of. Although I didn't know how much until after I left. Just like I didn't realize…" He leaned his cheek on Wes's prickly hair. "That I'd fallen in love with the woman who lived there."

Wes groaned, but he recovered quickly enough to ask, "With Zoey's mom?"

"Actually, with the whole family, but…yeah. With Zoey's mom. Who'd been married to my best friend, before he died. But I'd spent so long feeling like…like a fake, I couldn't wrap my head around what it was like to feel *real*. Does that even make any sense to you?"

A moment passed before Wesley slithered off the couch and went into the kitchen to pour himself some apple juice. That done, he came back into the living room and sat on the coffee table opposite Cash.

"You want to be with her, huh?"

Cash sighed. And nodded.

"So why can't you?"

"My own boneheadedness, for a long time. But now? You."

Wesley's forehead crumpled. "Me?"

"Yep. Because you and I are just getting to know each other, for one thing. And for another you yourself made me promise, *no girlfriends.* Remember? And the last thing I want to do is make you unhappy, pork chop. Or hurt you."

His gaze eerily steady, Wes took a sip of juice, then said, "You know what? I've wanted to live on a farm my whole life."

A smile pushed at Cash's mouth. "You serious?"

"Yep. Someplace where I can jump and yell and run all I want and nobody's gonna tell me to be still?" His shoulders bumped. "Sounds good to me."

Cash laughed. "Sounds good to me, too."

"So when can we leave?"

"You're really up for adding—" Cash counted "—five more people to this family?"

"I think the question is…are they up for adding us?"

"Probably so. But—"

"Dad. It's all good, okay? And you should've seen the look on your face—" he pulled an exaggerated happy face that made Cash choke out a laugh "—when I said I wanted to live on a farm. Which is totally true, by the way. *And* I could probably have a dog, huh?"

Oh, Lord—Al was gonna blow a gasket. But you know what? If something's right, things have a way of working themselves out, and whoever's voice that was in his head, Cash didn't know and didn't care. Because for the first time in his life he was going *to* something.

Not running away from it.

"How fast can you pack your bags?" he said, and Wes grinned so hard his ears looked like they were gonna pop right off his head.

"Ma-ma! Ma-ma!" His face flushed, Hunter crashed through the screen door, Bumble's crazed barking nearly drowning out his words. "It's Cash! He's back! And he's got... some kid with him! And a pup-py!" He grabbed her hand and jerked her off the sofa. "Come see!"

Sure either Hunter was hallucinating or she'd heard wrong, Emma grabbed her old sweater off the arm of the chair and followed him outside. A thundershower had passed through earlier, leaving a damp chill in the air and a tumble of clouds to catch the sun's final, brilliant color of the day. But that wasn't why she clutched the lightweight sweater to her neck, or shivered in the faint breeze.

That was because her blood had come to a complete standstill in her veins.

Cats scattered as Zoey streaked past, shrieking, "Cash! Cash!" and shrieking even louder when Cash swung her up into his arms to give her a huge hug. Then he set her down and introduced her to his son—a skinny little thing with sticky-up hair and a grin exactly like his daddy's, bless his heart, and Emma's heart turned right over in her chest. The kids, of course, already "knew" each other from their phone conversation, so Zoey then introduced Wes to Hunter before the pair dragged the kid off to the see the goats, trailed by Bumble and a bouncy, blissful ball of fur who looked like it might eventually grow up to be some kind of shepherd dog.

KAREN TEMPLETON   215

Then Annie opened the screen door to see what all the fuss was about, and Cash came right up on the porch to give her a hug, or she gave him one, it was hard to tell, saying she figured he'd eventually come to his senses, and then she went back inside like prodigal sons came home every day.

I'm dreaming, I've gotta be, Emma thought, right before Cash looked at her, and smiled, then stepped closer to lift a hand to brush the tears off her cheek she hadn't even known were falling.

Then he wrapped her up in those big, strong arms and kissed her like he would die if he didn't, and she thought, *Nope, not a dream.*

"You brought me a dog?" she said when they came up for air.

"Nope. Dog's for Wes." He grinned. "Did bring you myself, though."

Emma smacked his arm. Not hard. Just a little swat to help settle her emotions, before she tromped down the stairs and out into the yard, those emotions trailing behind like lost puppies, where she finally found her voice between the sunflowers and the cosmos.

"What...? Why...? You...?"

Okay, her voice, maybe. The words, not so much.

Cash shrugged. "Kid said he always wanted to live on a farm. Figured this one was as good as any."

Her brain on overload, Emma swiped at her hair, turning to watch her children with Cash's son, three peas in a pod after, what? Two minutes? She heard him come up behind her, her eyes closing on a sigh when his arms circled her waist from behind, and she thought, *Yes. This.*

"You said I'd always have a home here," he whispered into her hair, his breath warm where the pine-scented breeze was cool, and every bit as sweet. "Unless you've rescinded the offer—"

"Not a chance," she said, and he hugged her tighter against his chest, his chuckle rumbling through her, warming her soul.

"Then I've come home. To make a life with you, and the kids, if you'll have me. If you'll have us. The boy needs this," he said softly, kissing her temple. Driving her crazy.

"I can see that—"

"*I* need this." Gently, he turned her, his smile, his eyes full of everything she hadn't dared hope for. "I need *you*. You're my home, sweetheart. You and the kids and all this…it's where I belong." He pressed his lips to her forehead. "Where the real me apparently was all along."

Tears pooled in her eyes. "You sure?"

"More sure than I've ever been about anything. Except how I feel about that scrawny kid over there."

"But…what about your music? Your career?"

He let go, but only to sling an arm around her shoulders and lead her back to the porch, where he lowered himself onto the steps, taking her with him. "From somewhere in the deep recesses of my brain, I remembered some passage in the Bible, about when a man finds a treasure in a field, he goes and sells everything he has in order to buy that field?"

"It's one of Jesus' parables," Emma said. "The 'treasure' represents the kingdom of heaven, that it's worth giving up everything for."

"Well, all of this?" he said, sweeping out his free hand. "And you, and the kids…it occurs to me that this is about as close to heaven as this poor old cowboy's ever gonna get on this earth."

"I can't let you give up your music, Cash—"

"Or finish a thought, apparently," he said, squeezing her shoulders. "I finally realized it doesn't have to be an either/or thing. I can still write my music, maybe even cut an album now and then. And as long as it's on my terms, I might even play the occasional concert. We'll see. Country music's changed, but…so've I. If those two things mesh, fine. If not…" He shrugged.

His gaze shifted to hers. "Because music's not my safe place anymore. I don't need it to define me. It's what I do—or did—but it's not who I am. Not now." Wes's clear, bright laugh cut through the dusk, and Cash smiled. "Now I'm somebody's daddy." He lifted her hand to his lips, then pressed it to his cheek. "And I'd like to be somebody's husband, if she's amenable to that."

"Oh, yeah?" Emma said. Somehow. "Anybody I know?"

Chuckling, Cash shifted to slip warm, rough fingers underneath her hair, bringing their mouths together and making lightning crackle all over her skin. "Since you made me fall in love with you," he said, his eyes twinkling, "it seems only fair that you marry me."

"Is that so?"

"Yep. Heck, I'll even toss in an extra kid to sweeten the deal."

She laughed, and kissed him again. And then again, because she could. "I love you, too, Cash," she whispered. Grinning like a loon. "With all my heart."

"Is that a yes?"

"It is most definitely a yes."

"That's good, then. 'Cause I told Tess to take the house off the market." When Emma frowned, he shrugged. "Until that new master bedroom is done, Wes and me need someplace to hole up, right? And also," he said, shifting to dig into his pocket, "I'd hate to have to trek all the way back to Dallas to return this."

This being an emerald-cut diamond ring big enough, flashing in the sinking sun, to send a signal to Denver. "Holy mackerel," Emma breathed, trembling a little when he slid it onto her finger. She made a mental note to at least file her nails or something.

"It's okay, then?"

"Uh, yeah. But I didn't expect—"

"Shush, woman," Cash said, and kissed her again, before, his face creasing into one big, fat grin, he leaned back, his legs stretched in front of him. Then he gathered Emma to his side, where they stayed until it got too dark to see the kids, listening to the late-summer sounds, and their children's laughter, and each other's slow, steady, content breathing.

And Emma smiled, because Cash was right.

This was as close to heaven on earth as it got.

* * * * *

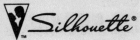
Silhouette®

REQUEST YOUR FREE BOOKS!
2 FREE NOVELS PLUS 2 FREE GIFTS!

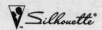

SPECIAL EDITION
Life, Love and Family!

YES! Please send me 2 FREE Silhouette® Special Edition® novels and my 2 FREE gifts (gifts are worth about $10). After receiving them, if I don't wish to receive any more books, I can return the shipping statement marked "cancel." If I don't cancel, I will receive 6 brand-new novels every month and be billed just $4.24 per book in the U.S. or $4.99 per book in Canada. That's a saving of 15% off the cover price! It's quite a bargain! Shipping and handling is just 50¢ per book.* I understand that accepting the 2 free books and gifts places me under no obligation to buy anything. I can always return a shipment and cancel at any time. Even if I never buy another book from Silhouette, the two free books and gifts are mine to keep forever.

235/335 SDN E5RG

Name _____ (PLEASE PRINT) _____

Address _____ Apt. # _____

City _____ State/Prov. _____ Zip/Postal Code _____

Signature (if under 18, a parent or guardian must sign) _____

Mail to the **Silhouette Reader Service:**
IN U.S.A.: P.O. Box 1867, Buffalo, NY 14240-1867
IN CANADA: P.O. Box 609, Fort Erie, Ontario L2A 5X3

Not valid for current subscribers to Silhouette Special Edition books.

Want to try two free books from another line?
Call 1-800-873-8635 or visit www.morefreebooks.com.

* Terms and prices subject to change without notice. Prices do not include applicable taxes. N.Y. residents add applicable sales tax. Canadian residents will be charged applicable provincial taxes and GST. Offer not valid in Quebec. This offer is limited to one order per household. All orders subject to approval. Credit or debit balances in a customer's account(s) may be offset by any other outstanding balance owed by or to the customer. Please allow 4 to 6 weeks for delivery. Offer available while quantities last.

Your Privacy: Silhouette is committed to protecting your privacy. Our Privacy Policy is available online at www.eHarlequin.com or upon request from the Reader Service. From time to time we make our lists of customers available to reputable third parties who may have a product or service of interest to you. If you would prefer we not share your name and address, please check here. ☐

Help us get it right—We strive for accurate, respectful and relevant communications. To clarify or modify your communication preferences, visit us at www.ReaderService.com/consumerschoice.

SSE10R

HARLEQUIN®

A Romance

FOR EVERY MOOD™

Spotlight on

─ Heart & Home ─

Heartwarming romances
where love can happen
right when you least expect it.

See the next page to enjoy a sneak peek
from Harlequin® American Romance®,
a Heart and Home series.

*Five hunky Texas single fathers—five stories from
Cathy Gillen Thacker's* LONE STAR DADS *miniseries.
Here's an excerpt from the latest,* THE MOMMY PROPOSAL
from Harlequin American Romance.

"I hear you work miracles," Nate Hutchinson drawled. Brooke Mitchell had just stepped into his lavishly appointed office in downtown Fort Worth, Texas.

"Sometimes, I do." Brooke smiled and took the sexy financier's hand in hers, shook it briefly.

"Good." Nate looked her straight in the eye. "Because I'm in need of a home makeover—fast. The son of an old friend is coming to live with me."

She was still tingling from the feel of his warm palm. "Temporarily or permanently?"

"If all goes according to plan, I'll adopt Landry by summer's end."

Brooke had heard the founder of Nate Hutchinson Financial Services was eligible, wealthy and generous to a fault. She hadn't known he was in the market for a family, but she supposed she shouldn't be surprised. But Brooke had figured a man as successful and handsome as Nate would want one the old-fashioned way. *Not that this was any of her business...*

"So what's the child like?" she asked crisply, trying not to think how the marine-blue of Nate's dress shirt deepened the hue of his eyes.

"I don't know." Nate took a seat behind his massive antique mahogany desk. He relaxed against the smooth leather of the chair. "I've never met him."

"Yet you've invited this kid to live with you permanently?"

"It's complicated. But I'm sure it's going to be fine."

Obviously Nate Hutchinson knew as little about teenage

boys as he did about decorating. But that wasn't her problem.
Finding a way to do the assignment without getting the least
bit emotionally involved was.

Find out how a young boy brings Nate and Brooke
together in THE MOMMY PROPOSAL,
coming August 2010 from Harlequin American Romance.

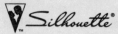